trusted him. They did not realize, and he could not tell them, that he was to be the instrument of their destruction, that no matter how sincerely Mercanton tried to undo his past, there was no way out for him.

There was no way out for Roger Chandler either, it seemed, caught as he was in a web of conflicting loyalties, but he determined that when the crisis came he would be prepared. . . .

And then he met Danielle, the beautiful, enchanting Danielle. From their first meeting he knew that this would be no casual, tinseled affair, that there would never be anything quite like this for him again. Their love was swift, immediate, devastating — a light flashing through the gathering darkness. . . .

Gordon Merrick understands men and how they react when the cards are down. He draws France with the etched clarity of a Remarque. He knows counter-espionage and writes of it matter-of-factly as a job, not a melodrama — a job in which a man is judged not by what he is but in cold blood by what he has done. His story will give you no rest, even when the last page is turned.

THE STRUMPET WIND

"How like a younker or a prodigal
The scarfed bark puts from her native bay,
Hugg'd and embraced by the strumpet wind!
How like the prodigal doth she return,
With over-weather'd ribs and ragged sails,
Lean, rent, and beggar'd by the strumpet wind!

The Merchant of Venice, Act II, Scene VI.
Shakespeare

THE

Strumpet Wind

by

GORDON MERRICK

William Morrow & Company
New York: 1947

TO

ROBERT BLAINE RICHARDSON

who contributed much more to this book than the

author would like to admit

AUTHOR'S NOTE

The characters of this novel are completely fictional and any resemblance they may bear to actual persons is coincidental. The same is true of the events described. There is, however, a wide gap between fiction and fantasy. Once upon a time, people were able to blunder through life without creating any serious difficulties, except for themselves. Once upon a time. Today, and for some years past, every man's smallest act has been laden with a heartbreaking significance. I have imagined a situation in which common human failures, common human virtues, assume a life-or-death importance. I have never known anybody whose life or person resembled that of Roger Chandler, George Meddling, Danielle Segher, Jean Louis Mercanton, or any other character in this story. To that extent, this is entirely a work of the imagination. But I have not imagined the world in which these people lived . . .

CHAPTER
One

I FIRST met Roger Chandler in the summer of 1944 on an LST bound from Naples to St. Tropez, in the south of France. The invasion of southern France, a relatively minor operation designed to support the major landing in the north, had started the day we left Naples. Our small ship carried a diverse and colorful fragment of what was known officially as the second lift.

The invasion of southern France was never regarded very seriously in military circles, possibly because of the rather comic loveliness of the terrain over which we were to advance. And also because the enemy had chosen ahead of time to let us have just about everything we wanted. But at that time it was our war and each of us had been getting ready for this moment over a period of many dreary months of training and preparation, discomfort and the special frustration of being a part of the Army without being allowed to prove it in any practical way.

It's difficult for me to give you a straight account of that trip. I remember . . . Well, let me put it this way. The weather was superb. Every morning the sun rose out of a placid sea like a promise of glory, and every evening it sank into a placid sea with a provocative splash of color. Our LST carried, as I said, a varied lot—intelligence officers and Red Cross personnel, civil government men and propaganda experts. It was a congenial group, and most of us had made the trip a number of times on peaceful missions, so it was easy to think of it as a holiday cruise.

We had slipped out of the Bay of Naples, past Capri, leaving the shadow of Vesuvius against the sky. We had moved in ponderous procession into the Mediterranean and past the precipitous shores of Sardinia and Corsica, straight for the holiday coast of France. We played cards and sang and talked about the wonderful restaurants in Theoule and Beausoleil, and what we would do when we got to Paris. We all had steady employment with a tolerant boss, so we were at ease and relaxed with each other, not maintaining the unconscious guards that men meeting as strangers retire behind under ordinary circumstances.

There's no reason why we shouldn't remember it that way. But there were other things. We played cards in bucket helmets and woolen OD's, a life-preserver hung over our shoulders. We sang as dusk came on, the gay tough songs that an army accumulates, but as the sun sank we stopped, and the ship was covered in hush and we stamped out our cigarettes as we passed into darkness, into protective oblivion. We traveled in convoy, a long procession that passed out of sight, of craft as diverse as the men they carried—transports and freighters and stern sleek warships and absurd bouncing little passenger boats that looked like the Boston night boat and seemed proud to have been drafted for the common service.

We were careful not to throw anything overboard because submarines have sharp eyes, and our jolly parade was lonely and touched with terror as night fell, and one by one our companions dropped from sight until we were alone on the great and ominous sea. Most of the ships carried a barrage balloon overhead, and during the day the sight of us all rolling, pushing, knifing through the water, was as cheerful as a handful of toy balloons at a county fair, but at night our own balloon rode over us like a silver sinister presence, pressing on us, independent but persistent, following us, a menace, a reminder. . . .

I slept throughout the three-day trip on a stretcher laid out on deck. I had picked it out of a pile below decks under a sign reading: "Stretchers must not be removed from emergency station." The lucky ones had found similar piles and we had set up our prizes on every bit of available deck space, on hatch covers, between ventilators, strapped against the rail. Mine just fitted the top of a stationary ammunition case, and there, imitating life like every good soldier, I set up my headquarters, received my friends, and conducted my business. Below me, on the deck, wedged between my ammunition case and the superstructure, I found another householder installed, a young captain whom I'd noticed several times during the day as we had embarked. Gaiety bubbled from him, and he was constantly the center of a laughing crowd, helping other officers board their gear or cheerfully giving a hand to the badgered enlisted men. Our intercourse had been limited to several nods as we set up our neighboring homes.

Shortly after nightfall, when we had already cleared the Bay of Naples, I pulled off my shoes and trousers, wrapped a blanket around me and stretched myself out on my improvised bed. I was already pretending to be asleep when I heard my neighbor rustling about in the dark beside me—the double thud as his boots came off, the faint pop of buttons being undone, the swish of trousers being drawn off. The stretcher creaked just below me and I heard the canvas stretch as he settled himself before he spoke.

"I suppose you know what you're sleeping on." He spoke softly in the dark. I peered down at him over the edge of my perch and caught the reflection of his eyes.

"You mean me?" I asked.

"Yeah. You know what you're sleeping on, don't you?"

"I don't know. How do you mean?"

"Well, that's a case of live ammunition. I just thought you ought to know."

"Fine," I said, trying to be bright. "You think it might go off?"

"No, not unless some planes come over. And then you could get off. But it's a nice idea, just the same." He had a fine low voice with a hint of laughter in it.

"Yes, I see what you mean," I said. There was a moment of silence, and then he said:

"My name's Roger Chandler." I told him mine and he reached his hand up to me. I shook it, and then I noticed he was wearing pajamas. It was so absurd under the circumstances I couldn't help laughing.

"You're making yourself at home, aren't you?" I said.

"Oh, the pajamas? Well, there's no harm pretending."

I was ready to let it go at that, but he was apparently in a talkative mood, and after a moment he asked:

"What outfit you with?"

I was grateful for the question, for my grey hair made

me conspicuous, and I liked being accepted on a basis of equality. Usually the question went: "What're you, Pop, one of those UNRRA characters?" I explained that I was with the Red Cross attached to Civil Affairs. He asked some more questions and I found myself giving a short sketch of my life.

I told him that I was an architect who had stayed on in Europe after the last war, working in many different countries. I had built the Bulkagov People's Recreation Center in Moscow, several housing projects in Cologne and Berlin under the Republic, and a number of public and private buildings in France. My wife had died in France in the second year of the war. The strain of living on short rations under the occupation had proved too much for her delicate health. I had been interned briefly by the Germans in a fairly agreeable concentration camp, had eventually been shipped home on exchange where I had begun the endless process of returning as part of America's vast war machine.

Chandler listened to my recital without interrupting, but I could feel his concentrated attention even in the darkness. As I grew to know him in the months that were to be so terrible for him I found this one of his most remarkable characteristics—his profound and genuine interest in the people about him.

As I finished he pulled out a cigarette, hesitated as he realized where he was, muttered "Damn," and pushed it back into his pack.

"So I guess you have a good many reasons for wanting to get back," he said.

"I guess all of us have our reasons."

"Do you think so? I have, of course. I know Europe pretty well, too, and I've seen what the Nazis have done, even to the people at home. But there're plenty of boys who've come along for the ride because they have to, and that's just about all it means to them."

"Yes, well, I imagine they'll have plenty of opportunity to find out as they go along."

"Yes, I suppose they will."

We went to sleep then, our balloon riding stealthily above us in the sky.

II

I saw a lot of Chandler during the rest of the trip. When I'd had a good look at him the next morning I saw that he was not remarkable looking. He was, rather, what we like to think of as typically American. He had a broad Nordic face with a rather blunt nose. His mouth was full but strong, in a way that is supposed to indicate sensuality but rarely does. He had light brown hair, streaked with gold by the sun, that sprang with a slight wave from a broad low forehead. His eyes, however, were unusual—set wide apart, which gave him a straightforward look, but faintly shadowed under straight brows, and very large. They were expressive eyes, deep and attentive, but, though he laughed easily, his eyes never smiled.

He was well made, broad and solid, but he moved with a grace that was not characteristic of his kind. His hands, too, fascinated me. He had big square palms and long delicate fingers, rather blunt at the ends. They were hairless and the skin seemed stretched taut over the bones, giving them the look of hard steel. His hands had power and a life of their own. When he touched something, his hands didn't slip over it, but met it and held it and curled around it as if he wanted to hold the world to him. He had immense charm, compounded of gaiety and simplicity and directness, and a mature repose which suggested a peaceful acceptance of life. But I noticed that when he lifted a cigarette to his lips his hands trembled almost imperceptibly.

He told me a good deal about himself during the trip, and more later when he laid bare his tormented soul, but he never told me what military organization he represented. I knew he was an intelligence officer, and I never asked for details. There were a good many intelligence outfits, all cloaked in alphabetical mystery—OSS and CIC and SCI and CID and PWB and possibly a few others. I never did get them all straight. Chandler had fallen into the work naturally because he spoke perfect French and pretty good Italian and German. His mother's family had been French, and he had gone to school for several years as a child in Chambery and Grenoble, and until just before the war had regularly spent his summers in the south of France and Italy. His father was a successful stock broker in New York and a member of a substantial New York family— not spectacular like the Vanderbilts or the Astors, but old and firmly rooted in New York social life. Young Chandler had been given a sensible education—Kent School in Connecticut after the brief period in France, and afterwards, Yale. He was only twenty-four when I first met him, so he had been too young to take much notice of the political forces boiling around him during his visits to

Europe. Too, good American education of the sort he had had is calculated to insulate youth against thought.

But his natural response to people, springing out of a warmly emotional nature, had led him to ask himself questions, and at Yale he had become deeply interested in Socialism and the labor movement. He had almost got himself suspended by joining a movement to unionize the campus workers. As the war gathered momentum, he joined all the inter-allied movements on the campus, and volunteered the moment the United States declared war. He graduated in 1942 and was commissioned directly into the Army. The next two years he spent in training—regular Army training and specialized training for the intelligence service, with a good many stretches of the dawdling that the Army provides to try the sanity of its personnel. At twenty-four, he had been at war in one way or another all his thinking life. He had thought war and talked it and written about it and practiced it. He, more than most, had investigated the influences behind it. He had had some experience of the many peoples and countries involved in it. He was an anti-Nazi, and he knew why. He didn't like racism and he didn't like the suppression of individual liberties, and he didn't like personal dictatorship. He really didn't like these things. It wasn't like some people sitting at home and reading the newspapers and saying, "Isn't this awful? Listen to this." He really didn't like them; they made him mad and he wanted to do something about them. He had even recognized certain aspects of the things he disliked in the life about him at home, and he wanted to do something about them too, when the time came.

It was a pleasure to listen to him. He made sense without

over-intellectualizing or taking the soapbox the way a lot of bright kids do. But although he was very sure of the things he was against, he was clearly confused about the things he was for. His talk reflected a negative rather than a positive point of view. He was, actually, equipped with a set of ideals learned from books. His background had stood in the way of their assimilation. He had never had an opportunity to test them. Yes, in spite of his obvious sound qualities, there were several questions in my mind that prepared me a little for the thing that happened later.

III

As I SAID, we had a lovely invasion trip. The days passed without any unpleasant excitement. We got up and stood in line along the rail for breakfast, and sat around and stood in line for lunch, and sat around and played cards and fussed with our gear, and stood in line for supper. Then we went to bed. The foredeck was closely packed with vehicles of all kinds, ambulances and trucks and jeeps, and a couple of mysterious-looking hearses that belonged to the intelligence groups. The enlisted men were assigned to the vehicles and lived and slept in them.

After the first day the whole deck looked like a dingy tourist camp. The men had rigged up hammocks and strung out clothes lines between the trucks. They sprawled about all day between the wheels, mostly in groups playing crap with thick wads of invasion lira, or centered around a kid with a mouth organ listlessly humming snatches of familiar tunes. Some just slept. There was a pair I particularly liked to watch. One was a sharp, tough little black-haired guy with a pimply face, who slouched half asleep against the rear tire of his jeep. The other was a big blond raw-boned kid with a dopey expression. He passed the days hunched over the little fellow, his big hands slowly, carefully fumbling through the little one's hair, intently searching, or squeezing pimples on the little man's chin. It was a gentle, painstaking labor, and went on with some interruptions almost the entire time we were at sea.

On the third day the word passed around that we were nearing our destination. It was mid-morning, and at first there was a good deal of stir among the enlisted men as they stowed their kit and passed cracks back and forth among themselves. "Who we gotta die for this time?" they called, and, "Come on, Wally, the German High Command has heard you was comin', so you gotta fix yourself up pretty." But after a while they quieted down and everybody just watched the sky, and the horizon straight ahead of us. I was playing gin rummy with Chandler. We faced each other across the cards in our helmets and life-jackets, our forty-five's strapped around our waists. I had been winning steadily, and was about to clean him out of his remaining lira when somebody called, "There she is." We both glanced up and I caught Chandler's eye. He just looked at me hard for a moment and I could see the muscles in his throat contracting. Then we laid down the cards and walked over to the rail.

There it was. A thin line of blue on the horizon. If you knew France you can understand a little of what it meant to me. I had lived in France off and on for more than twenty years. When the catastrophe came in 1940, I felt as if life had been unbearably diminished. There were

Frenchmen with us too, and their mood was contagious.
They had been exiles, and the return had been a long bitter
struggle. For a moment, we were part of a gallant and
breath-taking armada, bearing hope. Everybody stood
quietly and watched as the smudge on the horizon grew
and was transformed into the outline of those dear familiar
hills. A French liaison officer standing beside me murmured, "Enfin," and his eyes were filled with tears. None
of us knew where we were going; officially it wasn't even
acknowledged that our destination was France. But as we
drew near, all of us who knew the country were sure that
we were approaching some point between Marseille and
Cannes. After a while, Chandler stirred and I turned to
him.

"This makes the last two years seem worthwhile." He
spoke gravely, but there was an expectant, happy look in
his face.

"It looks pretty good," I agreed.

"I'm trying to remember all this," he said, "I'd like to
hold on to it."

"To cheer you through the dark days that lie ahead?"
I asked. We both laughed, and I noticed his hand tremble
as he lighted a cigarette.

We were soon in close enough for me to recognize the
long white line of the Hotel Latitude Quarante Trois, and
I knew we were going to land at St. Tropez. We were all
very busy as night fell and our LST lined up for her run
into the beach. We had to return the stretchers to their
positions and gather up our stuff and receive our debar-
kation orders.

It was late in the evening when I felt the ship grind to

a halt in the sand. We could hear occasional artillery fire, but the beach was quiet and we knew we were going to have an easy time of it. As I went down the ramp I saw Roger Chandler ahead of me, carrying a tiny lieutenant on his back—apparently some gag I didn't know anything about. I called a farewell to him, and I heard him answer as I struggled up the beach in the dark under my heavy pack. I didn't see him again for more than a month. By that time he was already caught up in his curious ordeal.

CHAPTER
Two

I

A FAINT whine, rising and falling like an unsteady pulse, passed through the house. In the kitchen, Marthe Mercanton paused over the stove and glanced up at the ceiling. Then, with a quick movement, she set down the pot she was holding and stepped to the kitchen door. There was nobody in sight. She turned and hurried out through the dining room into the small foyer and stopped at the open front door. She looked out into the courtyard formed by the wings of the house. It too was deserted. The muscles in her body seemed to go slack and she leaned against the frame of the door.

It was an early day of September, 1944. The sun was just rising over the corner of the house. For a moment she allowed herself to respond to the peaceful freshness of the vineyards banked in tiers beyond the courtyard. Impossible to believe that the Americans had fought their way through here just a few days before. And was it possible that somewhere nearby—Marseille, perhaps, or even Aix—these same Americans were going through files, collecting bits of evidence that would lead them to this door? That, too, was nightmare. Marthe Mercanton lifted her hand to her reddish brown hair and smoothed it listlessly away from her forehead.

She was not pretty. Her face was too long, her eyes a trifle too close together, the nostrils of her delicate nose too finely arched, her mouth too broad and humorous. The effect was bizarre, with a flavor of Toulouse-Lautrec. But the body was beautifully formed, with slender hands, full breasts and fine long legs. She was wearing a brightly colored cotton print dress, but her frivolous red leather shoes indicated that she was not entirely at home in the country.

The woman let her hand fall to her side. Her eyes were empty as they looked out on the brightening courtyard. Even now, in preoccupied repose, there was animation hidden in her face, and a gentle cleverness. Suddenly she was aware again of the faint whine throbbing through the house and she straightened herself abruptly. Her face focused and sprang alive with a wary alertness. She turned and glanced up the stairway and then went back towards the kitchen.

Upstairs, in a small room cut out of the attic on the third floor, Jean Louis Mercanton sat in front of a low chest of drawers, a pair of earphones on his head, his hand working a telegraphist's key. A small radio, contained in a sturdy leather suitcase, was set into the chest. The whine was louder here, the whine of sustained static. Mercanton adjusted one of the knobs before him, tapped out a burst of Morse code on his key, and then sat back in his chair. He listened for a moment, then lifted the earphones from his head and snapped off the radio. The sudden silence seeped down through the rest of the house. Mercanton

shook his head slightly, as if to clear his mind of the echo
of the whine.

He rose and detached the antennae from the set. He
placed the key in the suitcase and closed the lid. He tipped
back the radio unit and watched it disappear into the chest
like a desk typewriter. He walked towards the window,
coiling the wires of the antennae as he went. He lifted a
stone in the window ledge and placed the coiled wires in
a small hollow beneath it. He replaced the stone carefully.
Every move he made was spare and sure, as if he had
planned the routine for maximum efficiency. He glanced
quickly out of the window and then returned to the chest.
Two framed sheets of paper covered with typed transmission instructions were hanging on the wall above it. He
lifted them from their hooks and placed them in a drawer
of the chest. He went out the door, closing and locking it
behind him.

Once the key was turned in the lock, the Frenchman
seemed to spread and stretch. He made no movement. It
was simply that he seemed to breathe more easily, his body
seemed to grow less compact as the fierce control was
lifted. He stood for a moment in front of the locked door,
hesitating to go downstairs, absently studying the door key
dangling in his hand. He paused thus every morning at the
head of the stairs. He needed a few moments to prepare
himself to meet his family. He realized with distaste that
he was allowing himself more time every day for these
moments of self-preparation. It was ridiculous. It wasn't
as if he had done anything to be ashamed of. True, he had
been tricked. But that was in the past now. There was no
point in thinking about it any more. Why couldn't Marthe

realize that? Why did she always meet him with a look of regretful reproach? It was intolerable. Completely unjustified. Besides, a woman didn't realize how difficult it was to make decisions these days. The world was so confused. You didn't know where any act was going to lead you.

Mercanton raised his head and started down the stairs. His face assumed the proud, shut-in look with which he guarded himself from doubt. It was a well-modeled face, with high cheekbones, a long delicate nose, a thin hard mouth that was betrayed by a soft curve at the corners, attentive dark eyes, and a wiry shock of black hair above a high forehead. The hair was beginning to grey at the sides, but that was the only sign of age. He was taller than most Frenchmen, almost six feet, with a trim supple body. He had been born in 1900. He liked to point out that it was easy to remember his age, since he had grown up with the century.

II

As MERCANTON reached the foot of the stairs, Marthe, his wife, came out into the foyer to meet him.

"Everything is all right?" she said. It was as much an assurance as a question.

"Of course," he answered. He shrugged his shoulders, dismissing the question impatiently. He went past her into the dining room. The children were already seated at table, waiting for their breakfast. The little ones: Françoise, who had been born after the war started, and Pierre, who was eight. He went to both of them and kissed them on the cheek. They laughed in greeting and snuggled up to him. The older boy, Dominique, didn't look up from his plate. He sat hunched in his chair, jiggling his foot nervously. He was fourteen, high-strung and defiant. As his father approached his chair, Dominique seemed to shrink into himself. Mercanton hesitated behind him, his face settling into harsh lines, and then went around the table and seated himself. Marthe brought coffee and bread and they all ate for a moment in silence.

"I understand the Americans are establishing a number of offices in Aix." Marthe occupied herself with the coffee pot as she spoke, in an effort to appear casual.

"I have heard so too," Mercanton said. His tone was cold and painstakingly indifferent.

"I hear they've already made a number of arrests in the area," Marthe went on, looking across the table now with anguish in her eyes.

"Of course they have," Mercanton said angrily. "It is always so during wars. First one side is winning and then the other. It means nothing. The lucky ones choose the right side."

He set down his cup abruptly. Why couldn't she leave him alone? It was too late now, anyway. His pride rose in him. How dare she question his actions? He squared his shoulders and lifted himself very erect in his chair. It was a trick he had learned in the Navy. Ah, those were good days. Those were days when you could do your work without interference from the world. You knew the routine. You followed certain orders, observed regulations, and then you could do your work. You didn't have to get yourself mixed up in politics and questions of right and wrong. There were certain standards. You knew where

you were. That was the sort of life he had been prepared
for. . . .

* * * Jean Louis Mercanton was born in the village of Lam-
predoc, not far from Nantes in Brittany. He was the son of
petit bourgeois parents—a family of minor government officials
and small business people with the rather obscure pretentions
to the aristocracy characteristic of that dank and bitter corner
of France. He was early schooled in the doctrines of the region
—rigid self-control, a misty nostalgia for a royalist authorita-
rianism, and an almost fanatic nationalism. * * *

Sitting erect before his breakfast coffee, Mercanton's
mind was filled with an image of his father—a small, square
man with a huge mustache. He wondered what his father
would have made of the world today. It was just as well
he had died before the big changes took place. He had
always known that no good would come of a government
of the ignorant, the uneducated, men with no background
or breeding. And he had been proved right. To Mercanton, it was so simple. It was like a ship. There were those
that gave the orders and those that took them. That was
the way it had to be. . . .

* * * He had been just old enough to join the Navy in the last
months of the first World War. He had felt immediately at
home and decided to make a career in the service when the war
ended. By this time he had become an extraordinarily well-
disciplined young man, cold, immensely ambitious, with a fine
mind and a sensitive shy pride.

Mercanton attended all the technical schools the Navy could
provide. He discovered a talent for drafting and design, and
he had the kind of mind that likes to grapple with mechanical
problems. By the end of the twenties he was attracting atten-

tion with his improvements in warship design. As a sous-officier, he had gone as far as he could in the Navy without the classic Navy academic background. In the early thirties he gave up his uniform for a career in industry. He became interested in aviation and made notable advances in French design.

As the war started, he stood near the head of his field. He was prosperous, he was known and consulted by important men of affairs, he had been several times honored by the state, including nomination to the Legion d'Honneur. He had changed little with success. His manner grew perhaps a trifle more aloof. His sensitivity crystallized into a great protective pride in his own achievements. He drove himself unhesitatingly and grew increasingly intolerant of any indication of self-indulgence in others.

Mercanton married a girl from his own corner of Brittany whom he had known all his life, and who had been in love with him ever since he had returned from the war wearing a becoming uniform. Mercanton had never expected life to be adventure or romance. He accepted the forms and traditions of life without being aware of the dreams and aspirations of man which had created them. He married because it was fitting that he should have a home and children.

Marthe, on the other hand, loved Mercanton with an exclusive passion that filled her days with longing and rapture. She adored her husband, and did not know that by demanding nothing in return she was draining herself of her vital resources. She rarely questioned her husband's decisions and was satisfied that by her devotion she could win happiness for them both.

Once, Marthe learned that her husband was keeping a mis-tress, and found a photograph in his bill-fold to prove it. In a panic, she told herself that it didn't matter, that nothing could touch their perfect love. Her first impulse was to forget that she had found the picture, telling herself that she loved him in spite of such minor trespasses.

Reluctantly, she confronted him with her evidence only to find that somehow, in a way she never quite understood, she was at fault for permitting her doubt to lead her into such a petty violation of his privacy. Several days later, she could not resist looking for the photograph again. She never found it, and when she questioned him once more he treated the episode as a figment of her imagination. She was almost persuaded that the photograph had never existed. But she never felt whole again. * * *

III

MERCANTON poured himself another cup of coffee, adding just the right amount of hot milk. The inside of the cup was covered with a flower pattern. Mercanton knew the flower which marked the proper level for the coffee. Above the flower, he always filled the cup with milk. Very convenient. He glanced around the table. The children were thoughtfully munching their bread. Marthe's eyes were fixed on some point on the wall above and behind him. She did not meet his look. There it was again. Why did she insist on trying to make him feel guilty? Now that the Americans were here the situation certainly wasn't pleasant for him. Once he would have been glad of it. If they had only come sooner. But who could have guessed four years ago that things would work out this way? And who could be sure that they would stay? The others had been sure of themselves, too. And at least the others had some respect for the established way of life. They didn't encourage wild-eyed reformers and rabble theorists.

What would happen now? Revolution? And the end of everything that had been worth living for? He remembered the terrible June four years ago when everything had, in fact, seemed to be over. The fall of France had been a stunning blow. But the Vichy government had quickly emerged as the obvious salvation. France had been beaten before. There had been periods when she had had to adjust her destiny to the will of the conqueror. But these periods had passed and she had reclaimed her ancient greatness. And the Vichy government was composed of men who commanded respect—military heroes and leaders of industry.

As soon as the war was declared, Mercanton had gone to work on commissions from the government. After the Armistice, he had acted with scrupulous loyalty. He had delivered all his papers and incompleted projects to the authorities in Vichy. That had been the beginning of the terrible period—the months, the years of inactivity.

He had offered his services to the Vichy government. He had made regular trips to Vichy, determined to break through the barrier of polite dismissal. As the years passed, he was filled with a crushing humiliation. It was unbearable to sit idle. The money didn't matter. He had accumulated a considerable fortune during his successful years. But he was an established craftsman. He had worked hard to achieve his position. He would not be cast aside. Not that it wasn't understandable. The field in which he had excelled was in the tight grip of the Germans. One had to be patient. One had to support the government in its efforts to win independence through collaboration. He had heard of the Resistance at this time, but only as a troublesome group intent on upsetting the delicate understanding being worked out with the Germans.

Then there was Charlot. He couldn't remember exactly how he had happened to meet Charlot. It had been at Vichy. There had been a group of acquaintances in a café, and Charlot had singled him out. A gloomy, long-faced, gaunt man, in ill-fitting clothes. But he had been sympathetic. He had known of Mercanton's reputation. He had talked vaguely of possibly being able to help in some way.

Mercanton had been living with his family in Marseille at the time. After their first meeting, Charlot had called him several times at his home and they had had a drink together. It had been odd that the man had insisted on being known only as Charlot. No other name. But he seemed to have important connections in Vichy and Mercanton was not inclined to ask questions of anyone who might help him reestablish himself. It hadn't been until last winter, however, December of 1943, that Charlot had finally offered something definite. Come to Paris, he had said, I think I have everything fixed up. He would never forget that trip to Paris. . . .

*** Mercanton was at first profoundly shocked to find Paris in the hands of the Germans. He had seen direct evidence of the occupation before, because by that time the Germans had over-run all of France. But never had the outrage seemed so vivid to him. Only a Frenchman can feel completely the unique quality of Paris. Unlike other great cities of the world, which are simply independent phenomena, Paris is the complete expression of the people which made it. It is the sum of French tradition and taste. Paris is a little of every village in France. In their arrogant possession of the city, the Germans were violating the very core of the nation. Mercanton was enraged by what he saw, and felt an impotent compulsion to do something about it. If Germany had won the war, then Germany must be made to understand that it was to her own interest to allow France independent development in a new pattern of cooperation.

Actually, Mercanton had little time to think of these things. He kept his appointment with Charlot, and the next five days were filled with a succession of apparently senseless meetings, casual conversations and small dinners. The nature of the business for which Mercanton had come to Paris was never discussed. He did not know it, but he was being prepared for an easy seduction.

Altogether, he did not meet more than half a dozen men, but he saw them always in shifting combinations of twos and threes. These men seemed aware of his professional standing and spoke flatteringly of his important achievements and the great services he could perform for the new government. Everything was done for his comfort. He was never taken to public places, but was entertained quietly in handsome apartments with excellent food and wine. The men wore an air of prosperous well-being. Illusively Charlot guided the proceedings, always on the verge of getting down to business. To Mercanton, soothed by attention and respect, the past three terrible years of profitless struggle seemed very far away. He felt sure at last that his life had begun again.

On the sixth day, Mercanton was given an address in the rue de la Faisanderie, and was asked to be there at ten in the evening. "I want you to meet a colleague of ours. I think you'll like him," Charlot explained. At the appointed hour, Mercanton arrived for the rendezvous, to be met by Charlot and led into another handsome apartment, this one violently modern in the worst French style, but glitteringly magnificent. They went directly to a small room off the salon, where the agony of the décor was tempered to some extent by being limited in scope.

They had scarcely entered the room when a tiny man came scuttling in by another door—a grotesque little man with a great bald head. He wore thick-rimmed spectacles and his nose spread like a triumphal arch over his face. When he smiled it was as if angels had entered the room—it was a smile of gay and infinite tenderness.

"I hope you can ignore this frightful house, M. Mercanton. It makes me nervous, too." The little man spoke with whispered excitement. There had been no introductions. The three men seated themselves in chairs drawn close together, Mercanton sinking into one of leather and shivering bronze and wood carved in angular sunbursts. The newcomer made a gesture that included the room. "The French rarely make such appalling mistakes. But there. I believe we have made more important mistakes recently."

"That is surely true," Mercanton replied.

"You and I, we can say it because we love France. One must love in order to know. That is so, don't you think, monsieur? Oh, this ridiculous war. It does not appear to have ended yet. M. Mercanton, I have wanted to meet you for a long time. I am pleased with Charlot for having brought you. You have had a pleasant stay in Paris?"

"It's been a very pleasant vacation, so far," said Mercanton.

"Yes. You are beginning to wonder why you are here. Of course. I have reserved for myself the privilege of discussing it with you. You know something of radio, that is so?"

"I was trained as a radio operator in the Navy," Mercanton answered. "I know very little about the technical aspects of radio."

"I'm sure that is sufficient. You see, there seems to be no end to this war. We are constantly developing new methods, new techniques to meet every eventuality. We are just now embarking on a new operation. From everything I know of you, M. Mercanton, I feel sure you are the man we need to help us."

"But what sort of work do you want me to do?" Mercanton inquired.

"I'm afraid it will seem to you childishly simple. We want to provide you with a radio. We wish to instruct you in code. Then we want you to establish daily radio contact with us. You could send us—let us say, weather reports. Or anything else you wish. That's unimportant."

"But anybody with any knowledge of radio transmission could do that." Mercanton felt that the man was talking nonsense. Radio. Weather reports. There could be only one meaning . . . But no. That was impossible. He forced the unwelcome truth out of his mind. A shadow of disappointment crept over him. He had placed such hopes on this opportunity.

"No. That is where you are mistaken," the little man hurried on. "There are very few people we could trust with this work."

"But you can surely tell me why this work is so important. I should certainly know why I'm doing it." There would be some satisfactory explanation and the ugly suspicion in his mind would be removed.

"That is exactly what I cannot tell you. You understand these things." The man smiled his angelic smile. "The government must keep many secrets. If at any time there's reason for you to know more, Charlot can give you the details."

"Well, I don't know . . ." Mercanton began. He knew that too much was being withheld. But he was reluctant to insist on more information. At least, it was work. And, obviously, all these men considered it important.

The strange little man's voice whispered on insistently: "Of course, I know that money is of secondary importance to you. We work for the satisfaction of working, not just for gain, isn't that so? Still, I have authorized Charlot to fix a substantial salary as an indication of the importance we attach to this work. Well then, monsieur, I don't wish to force you to a hasty decision but this matter must be settled tonight. You will accept the proposition?"

Mercanton paused only an instant. He felt doubt pricking at him once more, but he refused to examine it. What could possibly be wrong with the situation? This was what he had been waiting for—a chance to serve the government.

"Yes," he said. "Yes, I accept." * * *

That was all. The interview had ended then. In the days that followed, Mercanton had received instruction in code and had been given a chance to display his skill at radio transmission. He had returned to his home in Marseille with a handsome month's salary in advance. In a few weeks, Charlot had turned up with the radio—a compact sending and receiving unit which fitted securely into a small suitcase. The set that was locked in the attic now. It had been good having something to do again. The work didn't take more than a half hour in the morning, but he spent much time tinkering with the radio and devising an ingenious workshop. Charlot had warned him that nobody must see the set. That had been odd. It was just an ordinary radio. Yes, there were a number of things about the business that even his well-disciplined mind could not overlook. The way he received his money. Always delivered in cash by Charlot. But he simply hadn't permitted himself to dwell on these aspects of the affair. He had congratulated himself on not allowing his imagination to run away with him. No need to trouble oneself with every wild possibility. His abilities had been recognized once more. The black period of inactivity was ended. Still, he hadn't felt it necessary to discuss the matter with Marthe. Women didn't understand such things. Besides, he had never talked to Marthe about his business affairs.

The early months of 1944 passed very agreeably, with the regular radio contact, the renewed sense of importance as Charlot turned aside his questions with repeated assurances of the great value of the work. Then, in the spring, rumors of impending Allied landings began to spread. Marthe took alarm for the children. Marseille wasn't safe. It had already been bombed. They must find a place in the country. Charlot had given his approval, provided the place was close to Marseille and the main lines of communication. That was curious, too. So they had found this vineyard, just outside of Aix, on the main highway leading north. Very comfortable. Too expensive, of course. But it was just as well these days to have your money in land. It was here that Charlot had paid his last visit. The Allies had landed in the north in June. Charlot had come early in July. . . .

* * * "I will not come again," he said. There was about him always a solemn calm that was singularly authoritative. He seemed quite unshaken now. "I'm going away. I must tell you a little more about your work before I leave. Our friends are counting on you."

"Well, of course, the more I know, the better job I can do," Mercanton said. Yet within himself he felt a sudden reluctance to be told too much.

"Yes. You see, everything that you have done so far has been practice. Now your work really begins. We will need information. Information of all sorts. Our government officials will probably have to be withdrawn from this area. Then we will need information about the British and the Americans. Information about their guns, their troops, their planes, everything."

"But I don't understand. Who will want this information?" There was the cold taste of fear in his mouth. He didn't want to understand.

"The Vichy government. The Germans. It's the same thing."

"You expect me to spy for the Germans?" Mercanton's brain was reeling with the truth he hadn't wished to comprehend. The whole conversation was unreal. It couldn't be happening to him. Why hadn't they left the facts unstated? It was so much easier that way.

"You can call it what you will." There was a trace of contempt in Charlot's voice.

"But the British? The Americans? The British were our allies."

"You think so? You think they have behaved as allies?" Charlot seemed to rouse himself slightly out of his gloomy apathy. "They have fired on our ships. They have killed our men. Who is our enemy? The Russians. Communism. The Germans are fighting that enemy. Our government is with them. What will happen here if we lose? You know very well. The Communist leaders of the Resistance will take control. The Americans? They will join us. You will see. It's only a matter of time before the Americans begin to fight the Russians too. They won't allow Communism to win. You know all this for yourself."

"Yes, of course," Mercanton said faintly. It was true. But

everything was so confusing. It was no longer possible to adhere to a few simple principles. One was immediately involved in a hopeless tangle of conflicting allegiances. Best not try to explore too far.

"Well, then," Charlot continued. "Shall we finish up our business?"

"Yes. Surely." Of course there was no question of backing out now. He was too completely committed. Besides, there were people who were counting on him. They had respected his reputation. And who could know who would finally come out on top? If only they hadn't forced him to recognize his decision.

"Very well," said Charlot. "You will continue your daily radio contact. You will gather all the information you can. From time to time, we will ask for specific details. That's about all. If at any time there's anything you need, just let us know and we'll figure out a way of getting it to you." He counted out three months' salary in advance. He said good-by. Then he went away. Months later Mercanton was to meet him again under very different circumstances. * * *

I V

THAT had been barely two months ago. So much had happened since. The second Allied landing, in the south. The trouble with Marthe. And always the gnawing restlessness. Was it fear? If Marthe would only leave him alone. Not prey on his nerves with silent reproach. He had never intended to tell Marthe. But after the second landing, so near at hand, the fighting had seemed to burst into the life of every individual. It was all about them. At any moment, it might be carried into this very vineyard. Marthe had seemed to sense danger in the house. One day, about two weeks ago, she had faced him with it. She had insisted on knowing what he was doing. He had never seen her so determined. He was unable to quiet her with evasions so finally he told her. Then it was worse. She had stormed at him. She had called him traitor and had accused him of dishonoring the whole family. It was absurd, of course. He had always been loyal to Vichy. Even the Maréchal had had to take refuge in Germany. But it was no use trying to explain all that to her. At last he had promised to destroy the radio if the Allies really occupied the region. Not that he intended to keep the promise. He was not a coward, to be frightened off by every turn of the tide. God knows, he would have liked to have been out of it long ago. It was after their stormy conversation that he had found Dominique lurking about in the hall outside the door. He had gone to the boy, but Dominique had pulled away from him, glaring at him venomously, and had rushed out of the house. Now the boy was growing more and more difficult to manage. And Marthe scarcely spoke to her husband. She simply looked at him with eyes full of pleading and despair.

Mercanton looked across the table at her once more. Her gaze was still fixed on the wall behind him. His coffee was finished. He was pushing his cup from him when he heard the sound of a motor climbing the drive and saw a big Renault bump into the courtyard and draw up just outside the window. He watched as two young men descended from it, both keeping their hands in their jacket pockets. One stood by the car, looking about him watchfully. Mercanton made a motion to rise, but the other, moving easily, entered the house by the open door and walked into the dining room.

"M. Jean Louis Mercanton?" he demanded.

Mercanton looked up at the tall young man. He was curiously foreign-looking, despite his cultivated accent. He had a broad face with blunt features, and his light brown hair was streaked with gold.

"Yes, I am he," said Mercanton. Marthe had dropped her spoon and was crouched forward, clutching the arms of her chair.

"I should like to speak to you privately," said the visitor. Mercanton rose, led the way into the living room, closed the door behind them, and turned. He found the young man standing with his back to the wall, his long fingers curved close around an automatic.

"I am an officer of the American Army," he said. "M. Mercanton, you are under arrest."

Roger Chandler stood face to face with his destiny.

CHAPTER
Three

IIIIIIIIIIIIIIIIIIIIIIIIIIIIIIIIIIIIIIIIIIIIIIIIIIIIIIIII

I

NEITHER man moved. Chandler studied the Frenchman.
He was struck by Mercanton's undeniable look of distinc-
tion. He was dressed for the country, with an open shirt,
stained trousers and a pair of wooden shoes, but he wore
his clothes with style. Chandler was astonished at his composure. He didn't seemed surprised nor did he make a
guilty effort to feign surprise. He simply stood quietly
with a look of abstracted preoccupation on his face, glancing from Chandler to the ugly automatic in his hand.
Actually, Mercanton was completely unprepared for this
moment. He had known that this might someday happen.
But he had known it only as an idea. His imagination
hadn't given it the substance of reality. He had protected
himself by forcing himself to think of his work as just
another job he had contracted to do. Now that circumstances had pushed him from business to melodrama, he
wasn't frightened so much as uncomprehending. After a
moment of watchful silence, Mercanton spoke.

"Won't you sit down, monsieur?" he inquired. He
could think of nothing else to say.

"Now look here, monsieur," said Chandler. "You can

save us both a great deal of trouble. We know you're a German agent. I want your radio and I want you to leave with me quietly. If you want to play games with me, I'll have to get rough."

"You will forgive me. I should like to sit down for a moment," Mercanton said vaguely. He sat staring at a table in front of him without seeing it. "I don't know exactly what to say to you."

It was true. In the films, spies were resourceful, ingenious, full of infinite guile. They never gave up without a pretty display of histrionics. He couldn't behave like that. He was an adult. He was a man of national prominence. The game was up. But it would take him a moment to make the acknowledgment that would condemn him.

"I suggest you tell the truth," Chandler was saying. "Also, it'd be a good idea to get your family out of the way. I don't want them mixed up in this."

"Yes, of course." Mercanton called out: "Marthe, please take the children upstairs to their room. Wait there for me. I'll be up in a moment." He still felt nothing but a faint uneasy bewilderment, like waking from a bad dream without being able to remember it. He asked: "Now just what was it you wanted to know?"

"I have very little time. I want your radio set. Where is it?" Chandler spoke with a quiet, brutal impersonality that cut through to Mercanton's consciousness.

"Very well. Will you come upstairs with me?" he said politely.

Without another word he led Chandler to the attic. He unlocked the door and led Chandler inside. He tipped back the top panel of the low chest of drawers and the radio slid out. He went over to the window, lifted the stone in the masonry and led out the wires of the antennae. He opened the bottom drawer of the chest and took out the neatly framed sheets of paper.

"These are my call signals and the Q code," he said.

"Is that everything?" Chandler asked.

"That's everything," he said.

"Good. Now I'd like to speak to your wife."

Chandler picked up the framed papers, wrenched the suitcase radio from the top of the chest, and the two men returned to the ground floor. As they passed the bedrooms Mercanton called his wife. They were in the living room once more when they heard her descending the stairs. She entered the room moving carefully, as if she might reveal a secret in her walk. Chandler spoke quickly, matter-of-factly, wishing to establish his authority from the start.

"Your husband is going with me. You will stay here, living as if nothing had happened. If you cause any trouble or ask any questions, you'll only make things worse for yourself and your family. just stay here and say nothing to anyone. I'll get in touch with you again in a few days."

The three of them stood awkwardly about the room, avoiding each other's eyes. Marthe remained near the door, her hands lifted in front of her but not quite touching, as if by moving she might destroy the desperate balance of their conflicting spirits. Mercanton stood idly in the middle of the room, preoccupied with a small cut on the back of his hand, embarrassed by the situation which still appeared to him startling and unreal. He searched his mind for a word or gesture that would bring them all back to an everyday level of behavior where he would feel at home.

Chandler, too, felt unsure of himself. This was the fourth such raid he had made since landing in France. The others had taken place in dingy apartments up narrow city alleys. There had been cringing suspects and hysterical denials, some bloodshed, and the harsh cathartic of destruction. This was different. He glanced at his automatic, aware for the first time that he was still carrying it. It seemed foolish—a false note of cinema-bravado. He slipped it into his pocket. He felt a sense of incompleteness, as if there remained something he should do.

"You understand, madame," he repeated. "You are to do nothing or say nothing until you hear from us." He waited for a sign from Marthe but she didn't move.

"Very well." He turned to Mercanton. "We have to go now. Are you sure we have everything?"

"Yes, everything that would interest you, I think. I'd like to pack a few things for myself."

"I'm sorry, monsieur. We haven't time." Chandler motioned Mercanton to precede him out the door. They hadn't taken more than a couple of steps before Marthe, still rigidly motionless, cried out: "You haven't the right to do this." Her voice was high and pinched, close to hysteria.

"I've warned you, madame," said Chandler. He guided Mercanton out the door and on into the courtyard where the car was waiting. In an instant, Marthe was beside him, her iron control dissolved into panting frenzy.

"Where are you taking my husband?" she screamed. Chandler turned on her. This was what he was prepared for. He felt sure of himself again. He stood close to her, his hands at his sides, his eyes hard with warning.

"You are to ask no questions. I promise you'll be sorry if you make trouble."

"When will I see my husband?" Marthe almost whispered now, her wide eyes close to the American's, searching for an answer.

"I can't tell you that. It depends on how you behave." He turned back to the car, picked up the radio and set it carefully into the back seat. He got in behind the wheel. Mercanton was seated beside him. The other young man was in back, his hand still in his coat pocket.

"Everything OK?" he asked.

"OK," Chandler replied. He swung the old Renault around in the rough drive and let it slide towards the simple wooden gate. A goat, tethered beside the road, flung itself into some shrubbery in idiot terror as they drove away.

II

ONCE on the main road to Aix and Marseille, Chandler reviewed his actions. His orders had been simple. Here's the name. Here's the address. Go out and bring this guy in without attracting any attention. That was routine. Roger's outfit always worked quietly, because several enemy agents might be in contact with each other, and a public arrest would scare off other game. It was a risk not to have searched the house, but after a thorough interrogation it was unlikely that Mercanton would be able to conceal anything of importance. It was a risk to have left the wife and children at liberty, but he had given Mercanton no opportunity to communicate with them, and fear would probably keep them quiet for the time being. Altogether, he was satisfied. It had been a good, clean, quick job. If, as was sometimes the case, the Germans had placed another agent to check on Mercanton's actions, it was unlikely that any irregularity would be suspected for at least a week. By that time, Chandler and his colleagues would have all the information they needed from Mercanton, and would be in a position to round up his associates.

Chandler didn't know all the details that had led to Mercanton's arrest. He knew that in the first few days of American occupation of Marseille, a number of names were turned in as having had some connection with Vichy. Among them was the name of Mercanton. There was some reason, based on special sources, for connecting Mercanton with the German code name, "Marc." That was all. It had been a lucky strike. But Chandler still felt vaguely uncomfortable. On previous arrests he had felt isolated from his victims by a wide gulf of hatred and fear. By failing to offer any resistance, Mercanton claimed attention on a personal level. The special ethic of war was no longer applicable. Chandler glanced at the man beside him, noticing again the fine profile strongly marked with intelligence and purpose. This was not the face of the enemy, cornered, contemptible with terror. Mercanton sensed Chandler's ill-ease. He was anxious to clear the situation of its disagreeable implications. It was unbearable to be treated as a prisoner, a criminal.

"You are French, monsieur?" he inquired.

"No. I told you. I'm in the American Army." Chandler spoke sharply. He was irritated by the tone of polite interest in Mercanton's voice.

"Oh, yes. Of course. But your French, monsieur. You speak like a Frenchman." In Mercanton's voice was the agreeable awe Frenchmen reserve for Americans who have mastered their difficult language.

"I've spent a lot of time here," Chandler said, reluctant to be drawn into a friendly conversation, yet unable to be rude.

"You lived in France before the war?"

"No. I went to school here for a little while. And I used to come here for vacations until the war started."

"Everything has changed since the war started."

"Yes. Things are changed." Chandler wished he could think of some way to end their talk.

"Tell me, monsieur. Is it customary in your army not to wear a uniform?"

"What's that?" Chandler had forgotten the incongruity of his civilian clothes. "Oh, no. Just in my service. We sometimes wear civilian clothes."

"Just when the work requires it?"

"Yes. Sometimes the work makes it necessary."

"It must be very interesting, your work."

"Yes, it's all right." Chandler said shortly. This was intolerable. The man seemed to regard the trip as a social occasion. Under the circumstances his attitude was almost indecent. "Look. I think you'd better not do too much talking right now."

The young man in the back seat leaned forward. He spoke in English:

"What's the matter? The son of a bitch trying to make trouble? I'd like to take a crack at him."

"No. It's OK. He's not making trouble," said Chandler. He took a stronger grip on the steering wheel and straightened himself, thinking of what he had to face in Marseille.

Chandler's outfit had established headquarters in Marseille, in a large private house on the sea. It was approached by a narrow, precipitous alley that slipped away from the Corniche just a few minutes' drive from the Vieux Port. It sat in a small garden behind high stone walls that seemed to have grown out of the rocky shore. Fog hung about it night and day, obscuring a magnificent view of the mountainous harbor, and the whole house seemed subtly stirred by the roar and pounding of the sea. It was just the sort of place that would have been chosen as headquarters by Chandler's commanding officer, George Meddling.

Meddling had a middlewestern background he didn't like to talk about and a frustrated feeling for drama. He was about thirty, a tall man with a superb physique and rather obvious good looks. He had a quality that was heavily male, overripe, decadent—a stifling quality compounded of the well-balanced characterless features, the full cruel mouth, the meticulous grooming of his whole body, the exquisitely tailored uniforms nicely calculated to reveal the broad shoulders, the full chest, the tapered symmetry of his waist and flanks. His civilian career had been shaped by his willingness to use his body to attain his ambitions. His narcissism led him to find satisfaction in the admiration of both men and women. He had been befriended by both sexes and had had a try at various occupations, from private secretary to a brief fling in Hollywood. But he had never quite succeeded at anything. He was filled with hate for a world that had denied him its rewards and had a seething contempt for mankind. He loved his Army job, and was good at it.

Most Americans were shyly embarrassed by the mumbo jumbo of intelligence work. Not Major Meddling. He had set up his headquarters with a relish for all the romantic details of spy fiction. The house he had chosen was ideal for his purposes—isolated, accessible only by the narrow alley, with long dark corridors of rooms where prisoners could be locked away. It delighted him when one of his colleagues once spent two days trying to find it. He had accumulated all the routine paraphernalia of the third degree, including spot lights and rubber truncheons. He never used the latter because wet towels were just as effective and caused less damage. He had a terror of inflicting serious injury upon anyone.

As Chandler approached Marseille, he was aware that the feeling of uneasiness was growing in him. He never enjoyed these sessions of interrogation with Meddling. And the man at his side, who now remained silent, had touched his sympathies. He was sorry he had had to speak sharply to him. But dammit, you couldn't chat pleasantly with a man one minute and beat him up, possibly torture him, the next. It was indecent. There was no other word for it.

Not that he questioned Meddling's methods. He knew that he himself was incapable of dealing with the men they picked up. He clung to the notion that if he approached a person honestly he would meet with an honest reaction.

He responded to people too simply. You had to be tough. You had to be merciless, relentless, without scruple. In short, you had to use Meddling's methods. Still, he didn't like it. It sickened him to see people stripped of all defense, grovelling like animals. He had too much respect for humanity.

Some people didn't mind it, even enjoyed it. Like Meddling. Chandler hadn't known Meddling for long. But instinctively, he disliked him. Meddling was too friendly, too eager to please, without ever giving any indication of possessing real feeling. And no one could go through a session of interrogation with him without being shocked by his brutality, while admiring his skill. No, Meddling was not the sort of man he liked to associate with.

He stole a quick glance at Mercanton, and saw in his face a look of rather wistful anxiety. As he guided his car through the rubble and destruction of the Vieux Port, he found himself wondering how this man came to be in such a predicament. From the Corniche he swung down into the narrow alley and drew up in front of wide iron gates, guarded by two American soldiers. They recognized him and pushed back the gates. He eased the car forward and parked in front of the path that led up through the garden to the grim house. There were more guards at the door, and inside several officers were loitering in the great dark hall. Chandler waved a greeting to them as he hurried Mercanton directly to Meddling's ground-floor office.

III

MAJOR MEDDLING was sitting at his desk, his back to the long French windows that opened onto the garden, when Chandler and his prisoner arrived. He looked up as the two men entered.

"Jesus Christ. Look what the cat drug in this morning," he said amiably. "Does this baby speak English, Roger?"

"I don't know. He might, but I don't think so."

"Well, look. Stick him out in the hall a minute, will you? Wait a minute. Let me look at him." Meddling rose from his desk and circled around the Frenchman. "Quite a kid, isn't he? Welcome to Heartbreak House, Frenchie." He stood close to Mercanton, insolently chucking him under the chin. Mercanton's face froze, but he didn't move.

"OK, George. I'll tell him to wait outside," Chandler said hastily. He stepped to the door and called. The young man who had accompanied him on the trip was waiting outside.

"Keep on eye on our friend for a minute, will you, Harry? I'll call you when we want him." Chandler turned and spoke in French to Mercanton, avoiding his eye. "This way, monsieur. We'll talk to you in a little while." Chandler closed the door as Mercanton was led out.

"OK, Rog. What's the story on this guy?" Meddling settled himself behind the desk. "Is he the one we're after?"

"Looks like it. I just walked in and asked for his radio and he handed it over. He has a nice house out in the country. I left his wife and kids out there."

"That's my boy. Great game, isn't it?" Meddling chuckled. "OK. We'll have to give him a good going over. I want to hear all about it later." Meddling called out:

"Harry, bring the body back." The door was opened and Mercanton re-entered.

"Now then, Joe. We are going to put you on ice for awhile. While you're locked up, you can think about your sins." Meddling knew enough French to get along but he always preferred to speak English in Chandler's presence. He was jealous of his subordinate's fluency in the language.

"We're going to have to lock you up for the time being," Chandler translated.

Mercanton made no answer. He stood uncertainly in the middle of the room.

"Nice chatty sort of guy, isn't he?" said Meddling. "And while you're waiting, you can pass the time writing a complete history of your life, who you know in the German service, names, dates, descriptions, the works. Tell him, Rog." Again Chandler translated. When he had finished, Meddling called out:

"OK, Harry. Come and get it." The young man called Harry opened the door and Chandler gestured to Mercanton to leave. The Frenchman hesitated.

"I have nothing to write with," he said. "Will you give me some paper and a pencil?"

"Oh, he has nothing to write with," Meddling said gently. He was waiting for an opportunity to "indoctrinate" the prisoner, as he called it. "Well, you can write with your blood, do you hear? Tell him that, Rog. He can write with his own goddam blood." He sprang from his chair roaring and placed himself in front of Mercanton. "Understand that, you lousy frog? You can write with your own lousy blood." He struck Mercanton hard in the face and turned back to his desk.

"OK, Harry. Lock the bastard up," he said, casually.

Late that afternoon, Meddling called Chandler to confer on the second episode in the "indoctrination" of Mercanton.

"Looks as if we pulled something out of our hats this time, Rog," he said as Chandler entered the big office. The monotonous stirring of the sea was an accompaniment to his words. "Look at this." He held out a sheet of paper patterned with a careful, delicate handwriting. "Some of our new guest's handiwork."

Chandler read through the paper. It was the description of a man Mercanton had met in Paris: "Little more than five feet tall. Bald, large hooked nose, thick spectacles, slightly deformed. Speaks excellent French. Smiles frequently. Very charming smile."

"You know who that is, don't you?" Meddling asked. "It's Hilburger, the Luftwaffe intelligence man. He wouldn't have seen Mercanton unless they expected big things of him."

"Does he give us any new leads?"

"Not a goddam one. Except a guy called Charlot." Meddling pushed forward a sheaf of papers covered with the same meticulous handwriting. "You better read it over. He says he was working entirely alone. He never knew any of the people he contacted. No names. Nothing."

"That's a hell of a note."

"Well, if he's holding out on us, you can trust your

daddy to get it out of him. The thing is this, Rog. The lads in Paris have been screaming for me to hold on to one of these babies. They want to give the firing squad a rest."

"What's the idea?"

"You know. They want to double one of these guys up. They want us to find somebody that stands solid with the Germans and keep him running. We give him the stuff to send across and the poor old Boche lap it up. The thing is, I think we might work the deal with Mercanton."

"What if he won't do it?"

"Are you kidding? He doesn't look like a guy that wants to die. Of course, we got to be damn careful. Nobody was around when you picked the guy up, was there?"

"Just the family. They live out in the country. It was a good quiet job."

"Well, we're all clear from that angle. If anybody knew about it, the story'd be around in no time and the whole idea would be blown."

"Sure, but what if he has some way of tipping the Germans off?"

"Don't you worry about that, baby. That's one of the things I'm going to find out. Don't you worry about that. Another thing. If we decide to do it, it'll probably be your job. What do you say? D'you think you could handle it?"

"Anything you say, George." Chandler tried to speak with the enthusiasm he knew Meddling expected of all his colleagues. But his mind was filled with reservations.

He was familiar with the process of doubling enemy agents. It was a device frequently used for counter-intelligence purposes. Through a controlled agent the enemy could be fed misleading information and a study of incoming messages might reveal much concerning the enemy's plans. But it was devious work. Above all, it meant associating intimately with a condemned man. For such controlled agents were granted a reprieve only for the term of their usefulness, and then they met the same fate as any other enemy spy.

Roger thought of Mercanton, and the feeling of uneasiness he had experienced that morning crept over him once more. Mercanton had commanded his grudging respect. The man's personal dignity was compelling. It seemed wrong to toy with him, to take advantage of his hopeless situation, even if he were an enemy. . . .

Of course, he was an enemy. He represented everything that Chandler was committed to destroy. Still, there was a catch. You fought the enemy, you killed him. That was clean and straightforward. This would be different. In this case, personal relationships would be involved and Chandler's whole concept of the obligation of honesty every man owed his fellows.

Chandler shied away from the problem. There would be plenty of other difficulties. It would be a lonely life. He would have to maintain a guard against everyone. He would have to weave a fine fabric of deception for the enemy. He would have to guard constantly against betrayal by Mercanton and his family. He would even have to isolate himself from his own colleagues, for the whole project would depend on absolute secrecy. He would have to train himself to trust no one. It was not a prospect he looked forward to. He hoped the plan wouldn't be carried out.

IV

At ten o'clock that evening Mercanton was brought into Meddling's office. He had been given nothing to eat all day, but he carried himself well, moving with dignity, a tentative expression of conventional interest on his face. The room was dimly lighted. Several filing cabinets and odds and ends of military equipment—bucket helmets, a dismounted submachine gun, half-emptied duffel bags—formed thick shadows along the walls.

Meddling was seated behind his desk, Chandler beside him. The young man called Harry followed Mercanton into the room and slouched against the wall. All three were now in uniform. Mercanton was directed to a straight-backed chair placed about four feet from the desk.

"Well, monsieur," Meddling began, of necessity speaking his clumsy French. "That was a splendid little autobiography you wrote for me. It is, of course, all true?"

"Certainly, monsieur. I give you my word of honor."

"Your word of honor. Now isn't that sweet." Meddling abruptly dropped his air of playful insolence. He was now stern and implacable. "There are a number of questions I want to ask you and I warn you not to lie."

"Of course. I'm anxious to tell you anything I can." If they would only get this thing over with quickly. If they would only realize that he was not a professional hireling, to be cowed into submission. He was a man of honor. He expected to be dealt with honorably. He couldn't stoop to lies or useless concealment. Couldn't they understand that?

"That's very wise of you." Meddling snapped a switch on his desk and a strong spot-light standing behind him cut into Mercanton's eyes. The Frenchman instinctively winced, and then looked back into the swimming glare, a faint smile playing over his face.

"But surely, this is a bit of fantasy," he said. "Surely that isn't necessary."

"You think that's funny, do you, you dirty spy." Meddling leaped instantly to his feet, rage strangling his flow of English and bad French. He lunged at Mercanton, seized him by the shirt and brutally shook him, knocking the chair out from under him. "That's very funny, isn't it? We'll have lots more laughs together, you and I. I'm a goddam funny guy." He ripped the shirt from Mercanton with obscene intensity and flung him onto the floor against the overturned chair. "You'll stay where you are, do you understand? You're not to move. We'll see how many laughs you can give us from down there."

Meddling swaggered back to the desk and sat down. The interrogation was ready to begin now—a savage flow of rapid questions, the answers checked against the written statement in his hand. Where were you born? Who have you worked for? Between what dates? Meddling had developed his technique as he went along, in North Africa, in Italy, and now in France, adding to it, perfecting it with loving attention. It had become a kind of exquisite formalized drama, refreshed and revivified each time with the consuming hate that pounded in the core of his being. Meddling was never able to satisfy the depths of his evil yearning. No matter what violence he permitted himself, there was always additional rankling energy to draw on.

Finally he lay back in his chair. He had completed the initial movement of his sinister composition. Mercanton hunched half-naked against the overturned chair. Chandler tried not to look at him. It was an absurd and uncomfortable spectacle, ugly and unnatural. Even Meddling seemed affected by it. He straightened himself in his chair.

"Pick that chair up, will you, Harry?" he said petulantly. "Put the bastard in it." Meddling was suddenly bored and weary. What was all this for? What difference did it make whether or not he wrung a few secrets from this man? Nobody told the truth, anyway, except to serve his own purposes. It was always a case of cheat or be cheated, beat the other fellow out before he beats you. That was it, of course. With a straining effort, Meddling directed his attention to Mercanton once more. But he felt sick and alone.

"Now then, monsieur, I want to know what your danger signals are—how you notify the Germans if you are controlled." Meddling spoke gently, persuasively.

"But I've told you," said Mercanton. "If there is danger, I sign my messages with my full name, 'Marc.' Ordinarily, I just use the first two letters of the name."

"Ordinarily, you just use the first two letters of the name. Yes, yes, yes. I know all that. Do you think we're children, my friend?" Meddling rose casually, and smilingly took a position just in front of Mercanton. "We understand now about using the full name. I want to know what other means you have. What other signals. Who you make personal contact with in case of need."

"There is nothing else. I know nobody to contact."

"This is very tiresome. What about Charlot? Have you forgotten Charlot?" Meddling still spoke with mocking gentleness.

"Oh, yes, of course. Charlot. But I tell you, I don't know Charlot. He used to come to me. He may come again. I can't tell about that."

"No, of course. You can't tell about that." Smiling amiably, Meddling struck Mercanton across the face with the full force of his open hand. "But you mustn't be forgetful, you understand. Now, let me ask you once more. Who are you in contact with?"

"But there's . . ."

"Who are you in contact with?" Meddling struck once more with his open hand. He repeated the question over and over again, with rising intensity, punctuating it each time with a blow. Mercanton rocked in his chair, gripping the sides of it hard with his hands. Finally, his eyes clouded with indignation, he managed to speak:

"How can I answer when you are doing this?"

"Good. I'll stop and you can talk all you want." Meddling was breathing a little heavily from his effort.

"I swear to you, I've told you everything I know."

"Christ damn it, you'll think of more before I'm finished," Meddling shouted. He smashed his fist into the side of Mercanton's face. He strode furiously over to the side of the room, picked up a towel, dipped it into a pail of water and coiled it into a tight bludgeon. He picked up one of the rubber truncheons in his other hand and walked back into the island of light in the center of the room. Mercanton was bowed in the chair, trying to stop a flow of blood from his nose. It had run down onto his trousers and was forming a little pool between his feet.

"All right, goddammit. This is going to hurt you a hell of a lot more than it will me." It was the sort of remark

that established Meddling as a good guy with his colleagues. He laid the rubber truncheon on the desk. He
rolled up one sleeve, uncovering a finely muscled arm, took
a quick step forward and brought the rolled towel expertly
down on Mercanton's bare shoulders. The thin sharp pain
made the Frenchman leap from his chair. Meddling
tripped him and brought him to his knees.

"OK. That's where you're going to stay for awhile,"
Meddling grunted. His arm was working rhythmically
now, up, snap, a quick turn of the wrist, down. The pain
licked over Mercanton's body in short little spasms, high
provocative pain, snapping his body this way and that.
The room was absolutely still except for the whish and
crack of the towel and the occasional quick gasps of Mercanton's breath.

Chandler remained at the desk, his head averted over his
crossed arms, his long fingers digging into his forearms.
High on the opposite wall above them all, the soaring
shadow of Meddling and his flailing arm kept heroic time
to the grotesque inquisition. From time to time, Meddling
would pause to inquire: "Have you thought of anything
to tell me yet, pal?" Mercanton would shake his head and
the methodical beating went on. After about twenty minutes, Meddling suddenly dropped the towel, caught Mercanton hard in the stomach with his knee, and strolled
back to the desk. Mercanton lay on the floor, breathing in
long shuddering gasps. Big red welts were beginning to
rise all over his upper body. Blood was clotted under his
nose and on his chin, and there were smears of blood on
his trousers.

"OK, Harry. Put the son of a bitch back in his cage."
Meddling sat down and carefully unrolled his sleeve.

Harry moved forward and leaned over Mercanton. He
nudged him on the shoulder. "Come on, Mac," he said.
His voice was strangely muted. He put his hands under
Mercanton's armpits and lifted him to his feet. The
Frenchman stood unsteadily, leaning against the soldier,
bent slightly at the middle. He made a vague gesture for
his shirt. Harry picked it up and put it around Mercanton's
shoulders. He started towards the door, almost dragging
Mercanton with him. After a few steps, the Frenchman
seemed to pull himself up, and walked painfully out the
door a little in front of Harry, still bent over, holding his
shirt around his shoulders.

Meddling pulled a small comb out of his hip pocket.
The room was still except for Meddling's heavy breathing
and the sound of the comb passing through his hair. Even
the sea sounded remote and appeased. Chandler sat beside
the desk, his arms folded on it, his head bowed. He didn't
want to look at Meddling for a moment. It would be all
right in just a moment. Why should he be so upset by this
mild display of brutality? It might have been much worse.
The enemy would have regarded this as mere child's play.
He remembered some of his radical friends laughing at his
"bourgeois sensibilities." He would never learn that gentle-
manly methods were outmoded, they had said. Was that
it? Had his gentle background left him unequipped to face
today's realities?

Sure, this was a fight to the finish. It didn't help to have
too many scruples. You just made yourself more vulner-
able. But if you threw all your principles overboard, what

was left to fight for? He didn't believe that ends always justified the means. Especially when lots of people didn't agree about the ends. What were they all fighting for? He felt sure that everything would seem cleaner, more honest somehow, if there were a final, generally accepted answer to that question. Now Meddling stirred beside him and started to speak.

"Well, there's your case, Rog. I think he's telling the truth. But it's the goddamdest situation I've run into. They usually cover a man with at least one live contact to keep an eye on things. The radio traffic bothers me, too. He ought to have more than one way of telling them if something funny's up."

"Maybe they have a lot of confidence in this guy." Chandler made an effort to bring his mind back to the business at hand.

"Yeah, it could be that. Look, Roger, go through this stuff again, will you? I want to know what you think. We've got to decide what to do." Meddling handed over Mercanton's carefully written statement. He reached into the bottom of his desk and pulled out a bottle of cognac and two glasses. He handed Chandler a drink and sipped one himself while Chandler leafed through the familiar pages.

V

ROGER knew the details of Mercanton's life by heart now. It was the section on the radio transmission that particularly interested him. Mercanton had made almost daily contact with his parent station for more than six months. He identified himself with call letters which were different for

each day of the month. His messages were encoded in a
German military code which Chandler had been taught in
Washington. Transmission procedure was carried out in
the international Q code—QRU for "No message today,"
QSM for "Please repeat message" and so on. Chandler was
amused to see that some American radio mannerisms had
been adopted by the Germans, so that anybody listening in
on Mercanton would suppose he was hearing an American
transmission.

Mercanton had no copies of his messages, but had sum-
marized those sent since the Allied landing: a report of
several large troop convoys on the road going north out
of Aix, a description of Seventh Army shoulder insignia;
nothing of any importance. There it all was, with Mercanton's neatly mounted original instruction sheets to suggest
that nothing had been concealed. Roger studied the sheets
carefully for flaws. If Mercanton were to be allowed back
on the air, there could be no slip. One deviation from regular procedure would instantly arouse enemy suspicion.
Everything looked almost too simple, too straightforward,
to be convincing.

"Well, George, I guess it's all OK," Chandler said finally.
"If we're going to run this guy, we ought to take him
right back tomorrow morning so there won't be any break
in his contact."

"That's what I was thinking. He's got a six-thirty schedule, hasn't he? Well, I'll go out there with you to look
things over. We can see how things go the first time, and
then decide whether to go on with it. I think it'd be better
if I go out there with you."

"Yeah, sure," Chandler said without enthusiasm. "D'you think he ought to send a message tomorrow?"

"No, why bother? Just let him make his contact. That's the thing about this set-up. We don't have to send anything important at first. Start him slow and build him up solid. Paris has given me an okay to send any local stuff. You know, just chicken feed. Paris will give us the big deception stuff later. But it's a tricky business, Rog. You've never handled a case like this, have you?"

"No, but I've read a lot of case histories."

"I'm sure you can do it OK. For God's sake, remember one thing. Don't let the guy get any idea what's going to happen to him. Let him think that if he does this job he'll get off easy. Otherwise, he's apt to give you a lot of trouble."

"I suppose he'll be shot, like the others." How extraordinary, Chandler thought, to speak of a man's life so casually.

"Sure. But don't let him know that. You've got to give him an incentive to work for us. Another thing. I see this guy has plenty of money. Don't let him use it. I'll give you money to take care of the lot of them. Keep his bank account frozen. We'll take it over along with all the rest of his property when we're through with him. Got all that straight?"

"Sure. It looks as if it'd be pretty clear sailing."

"I know you can handle it. It's a great game isn't it?" Meddling laughed and drained off his brandy.

VI

Upstairs, Mercanton stood in the dark in the middle of his small bare room, looking out the window. There, out along the rocky shore, on the long sweep of the harbor where the moon was dimly reflected on a cluster of white-faced houses, out there had been his home. He had lived out there with his wife and children. His wife. His mind stumbled over the word, trying to clothe it in flesh and blood. His children. Had lived with his wife . . . and his children. And this was the way it all ended. He was stiff all over. Pain throbbed in his shoulders and down his back. His face had suddenly assumed an existence of its own, independent and unfamiliar with pain. His mind was heavy and clogged with nerveless despair.

How could this have happened to him? Where was the flaw in the structure of his beliefs that had led him to this? He stood where Harry had left him, too broken and sore even to reach the bed. His mind searched slowly for the principle that had betrayed him. He heard his father's voice: "You must work, Jean Louis. You have inherited a fine tradition. You must work to uphold it. You must work." He had worked. And well. Was there anything wrong with that?

"I am a Chevalier of the Legion d'Honneur," he told himself. "I am a Chevalier of the Legion d'Honneur." But the words held no magic. He remembered with what satisfaction he had received the honor. But it offered him no comfort now.

He thought of Marthe as she first came to him, her eyes alight with adoring wonder. He had given her a good home. He had been a good father to their children. At first, she had seemed to want something more of him. It had bothered him for awhile. He had been too busy to find out what it was.

He had believed in his country, too. He had remained loyal to his government even in the black days. There was nothing else. That was his life. How many men could point to greater achievements? For an instant, the block in his mind seemed to give way and a rushing, choking agony surged up from within himself, sending tears stabbing at his eyes. Discipline, he said to himself. He tensed himself, trembling with the effort, and the moment passed. Discipline. It wouldn't be so bad if it were over with quickly. He wouldn't mind so much if it were quick. It would be the long days and nights of waiting with nothing to take his mind off himself that he couldn't bear.

Mercanton was still looking out the window when Chandler entered. He heard the sound of the key turning and the door open and close, but he did not turn his head.

"You'd better get some rest, monsieur," said Chandler softly. "We're taking you home tomorrow morning early." He paused, but Mercanton made no response.

"It's all right. You're going to make your regular contact tomorrow. You may be able to do some very important work for us." Chandler paused again, but still Mercanton made no sign. "You'll need some rest. Good night."

Mercanton turned, and in the half light he could see the large eyes of the American fixed on him. As he looked into them, he could see the expression drain from them but too late to conceal an unwilling response.

"Yes. I'll get some rest now," he said.

Mercanton watched the young American go out and close the door. He listened to the turn of the key in the lock. He stumbled to the bed and sat down. His mind was clear now, and cold.

Of course. Important work, the young man had said. He could still do important work. They had beaten him. They had humiliated and degraded him. But they could not dispense with him. He sat very still, allowing his mind to clear of the corrosive uncertainty of a moment ago. . . .

He had been right all along. It was to go on as always. Relief soothed the pain in his body, but he was filled with a sudden fierce anger. He had been a fool. A moment ago he had felt his world dissolving. He had allowed himself to doubt, to question the traditions on which he had built his life. He had put himself on a level with the idle dreamers. Obviously, life was to be taken as you found it. He would never permit himself such weakness again.

CHAPTER

Four

I

AT FIVE O'CLOCK the next morning, two cars drove through the heavy iron gates of the gloomy house by the sea, struggled up the twisting alley onto the Corniche, and fell into place in the rumbling stream of military traffic heading north to the fighting front. Chandler was still driving the shabby Renault, Mercanton seated beside him, the young man called Harry in the back seat. The Americans were once more wearing civilian clothes. Mercanton had bathed his face and, aside from a few puffy bruises, looked fit and rested. Meddling followed, alone in a glittering Rosengarde. He, too, was dressed in civilian clothes.

Just beyond Aix, the two cars turned off the main road to Avignon onto a small country road that led past vineyards and simple stone farmhouses. Chandler was seeing this bit of country for the first time. The day before, he had been too absorbed in his job to look about him. It was curiously appealing country—at the same time gentle and vaguely forbidding. Small plains, set with vines in neat rows in the red earth, were broken by low hills shaped with terraces of vines and silver olive trees. Beyond them, the rocky unproductive hills rose grey and agonized. On

the far horizon, blue mysterious ranges were painted on
the taut silk of the sky. The mark of man's orderly creative
hand lay everywhere—in the clear lines of the houses with
their coats of whitewashed plaster and their red tile roofs,
in the casual symmetry of the tiny towns clustered on
nearby hilltops, in the geometric fields and the tumbling
grace of the terraces. Man had possessed this land—the bar-
ren hills that lay just beyond its rich order seemed tragic
in their exclusion.

The two cars bumped disconsolately down the dirt road,
which soon deteriorated into a deeply rutted cart track.
In front of wide gates set in stone posts, which carried the
banal name of the property, "La Violette," on small
wooden signs, they drew up. Mercanton got out and
opened the gates. The drive led up into a fold of the hills
and they had almost entered the courtyard before the
house was visible.

The French have always built well. In the south, the
houses are simple and unadorned, with thick stone walls to
keep out the heat and almost flat roofs of tile. The Mercanton house was typical of its kind, though considerably
larger than most. It was built in an el, and one wing housed
the animals and farm equipment. Its plaster covering was
tinted a pale yellow, with green blinds standing guard at
the doors and windows. A spring bubbled up into an
ornate font in the courtyard. Two great oaks protected
it from the blazing sun. A paved terrace, covered with a
trellis of flowering vine, ran along one end of the house,
looking down through the break in the hills onto the plain
below. The house was set into a hill and the terraced vineyards rose all around it, but set back from it so that the

feeling was not one of enclosure, but rather of protected isolation.

Marthe Mercanton stood surrounded by chickens, a bowl of grain in her hand, as the two cars drove into the courtyard. She quickly spilled the contents of the bowl onto the ground and walked cautiously forward as Chandler stepped out of the lead car. The early-morning sunlight lay about them in fresh pools of cool light.

"Bonjour, monsieur," she said.

"Bonjour," Chandler responded gravely.

Her eyes moved slowly over to Mercanton and held him silently. Her face was tight with nervous exhaustion, and her wide mouth moved faintly several times as if she wished to speak. As she became aware of the bruises on her husband's face, the expression in her eyes sharpened, and her mouth settled into a harsh line. Her breath began to come more rapidly.

"Bonjour, my dear one," she said at last.

Chandler moved back to the other car, where Meddling was still sitting, regarding the house.

"Not bad," Meddling said in English. "Not bad at all."

"No English here," Chandler muttered hastily. Meddling climbed out of his car and the two walked back to where Mercanton was helping Harry unload the radio. Marthe was still standing beside the car, her eyes fixed on Mercanton.

"We'd better hurry." Chandler glanced at his watch. It was almost six-fifteen. He was tense with anticipation. "You stay here in the car, Harry. Don't talk to anyone." He turned to Marthe and lowered his voice. "There's no one in the house?" She shook her head.

Mercanton led the way into the house and up to the attic. Chandler and Meddling followed, carrying the radio and the signal papers. Mercanton installed the set on the low chest of drawers, led in the antennae and plugged the set into a wall socket. He hung the framed papers on the small hooks in the wall in front of him. He took a big old-fashioned gold watch out of the top drawer, wound it, and placed it beside the radio.

He sat hunched over the chest, his eyes on the white face of the watch. Meddling sat a little behind him, and to one side, watching every move he made. Chandler stood away from the other two, beside the window, his automatic in his hand, glancing out from time to time onto the driveway below. He held his head cocked slightly to one side, listening for any unexpected sounds in the house.

Just as the hands of his watch touched six-thirty, Mercanton straightened himself in his chair, lifted his hand and began to tap out his call signal for the day. "PLB," he tapped. "PLB PLB PLB." Over and over again, his square, blunt fingers working the key expertly. At six thirty-five, he stopped tapping, adjusted his earphones carefully on his head and began to twist the dial, searching for the answering call of his parent station.

From across the room, Chandler could clearly hear the nervous rhythms, the whines and sudden snarls of the burdened air. After five minutes, Mercanton resumed his signalling. By six forty-five, he was bent over the machine as if he would tear some response from it, a look of concentrated fury in his face. Both Chandler and Meddling were inclined slightly towards him, watching his performance intently. At a few minutes past seven, he wrenched the earphones from his head, snapped off the radio, and stood up.

"It's no use. They aren't listening," he said.

"That's tough luck for you, my friend," said Meddling.

"I don't understand you, monsieur," said Mercanton. There was resentment in his voice. Did they expect him to perform miracles? "I've done everything possible. We'll just have to try tomorrow."

"Has this sort of thing happened before?" asked Chandler. Mercanton hesitated for an instant.

"Yes, once or twice," he lied hastily. "But not for some time."

"Well, maybe you ought to go on trying now," Chandler suggested.

"It's no use. My period is from six-thirty to seven. They wouldn't be listening for me after seven."

"Do you have any idea what might be the matter?"

"I can't imagine. Something has possibly gone wrong with the radio. I don't know. Maybe I can . . ." Mercanton looked at the set and shrugged his shoulders helplessly.

"Come on, Rog," Meddling interrupted. "Let's go down and talk this thing over. Bring the radio."

The three returned to the ground floor. Marthe was waiting for them in the tiny foyer. As they reached the bottom of the stairs she glanced from one to the other, and knew immediately that something had gone wrong.

"Will you have some breakfast, messieurs?" She observed the formulae of polite usage as the last desperate defense against panic. Actually it would have been easier for her to spring at these strangers and tear at their faces with her hands than to ask them to sit at table with her.

The two foreigners nodded assent to her invitation, and they all filed into the dining room. Chandler caught a glimpse of the children in the kitchen beyond as they entered the room. Marthe followed the direction of his eyes and guessed what he was thinking.

"I've told the children to go out," she said. "You'll have complete privacy here." She went to the kitchen and herded the children out the back door. She returned in a moment with a bowl of fresh figs, pots of coffee and hot milk, and a long loaf of bread. The three men helped themselves in awkward silence and thoughtfully began to eat. Marthe stood at the end of the table watching them.

"Is my husband going to stay here now?" she asked at last. Tears sprang to her eyes as she started to speak, and her question ended in a little strangled gasp.

"We aren't sure yet," said Chandler with an attempt at kindness. "This situation isn't pleasant for us, you know."

"Yes, of course. But it's hard, you understand." Marthe's tears were flowing freely now. "It's hard not knowing. I've tried . . . there are the children, and . . ."

"Oh, for Chris' sake, shut her up," Meddling growled. "Tell her we'll blow her old man's brains out if she doesn't shut up."

Marthe recognized the ugliness in his voice. She checked herself, hastily picked up the empty coffee pot and returned to the kitchen. Meddling watched her go, a little contemptuous smile flickering across his tiresomely handsome face.

"I'm afraid I frightened the lady," he said. He leaned back in his chair and stretched. "No reason why we shouldn't speak English now, Rog. What d'you think about this thing? Shall we drop the whole idea and throw our gentleman friend to the lions?" He indicated Mercanton who sat contemplating his empty coffee cup.

"Do you think we ought to?" Chandler asked. He wished that Meddling would go. His coarseness was an embarrassing contrast to the simple dignity of these French people. Unconsciously, he was drawn to the couple out of his antagonism to Meddling. He felt sure he could handle the case better if he were left alone. "There might be something funny here. I think we ought to hang on for awhile and try to find out what the set-up is. The case looks good. If we can make contact we might have something."

"Yeah. Well, maybe you're right." Meddling was bored with a case once past the detection and interrogation stage. "What do you think? You want to stay on here a couple of days and see what happens? You ought to be comfortable, anyway."

"Sure. I'll be OK." Chandler looked around the room. The sun was just beginning to light the pale washed plaster walls and strike reflections from the simple, heavy darkwood furniture. Bowls full of leaves and late flowers were set about, and a few pieces of fine china were ranged on the sideboard. It was a pleasant room. Chandler felt at home here. Meddling spoke again.

"D'you think you can handle this thing alone, Rog? I could leave Harry with you."

"Lord, no! Nobody ought to be here who can't pass himself off as a Frenchman."

"That's what I was thinking. Well, all the boys are busy. I can't spare any of them. If you run into anything, you can always stick Junior in the car and come on back to town. Have you got your papers?"

"Yes, I've got them." Chandler felt for them in his pocket. When he had first landed in France he had been provided with a false identity card in the name of Roger Dulin, and a French Ordre de Mission permitting him to travel in the old Renault.

"Well, I guess that's it." Meddling stood up. "I probably better get the hell out of here. Take it easy. Don't try to win the war. You better keep in touch with me by phone from Aix. Come on in as soon as anything turns up."

Meddling left the room without looking again at Mercanton. Chandler followed him to the door and watched as Harry transferred from the Renault to Meddling's car. He waved as the big shiny Rosengarde turned and coasted down the driveway. Thank God, he thought to himself, that's over. He was filled with a surprising satisfaction as he realized that he was in sole charge. His thoughts moved back to the people inside. Strange. You couldn't help liking them. They'd come through all this damn well. He turned and walked back into the dining room. Mercanton sat at the table where Chandler had left him. Marthe stood behind him near the kitchen door. They both regarded him expectantly as he entered.

"Your colleague has gone?" asked Marthe.

"Yes, he's gone. I'm going to stay."

"My husband will stay here now too?"

"Yes. For awhile, at least." As Chandler spoke, Marthe closed her eyes in sudden relief, and her face lighted for the first time since Chandler had seen her. She moved forward quickly and placed her hand lightly on Mercanton's shoulder, as if she felt safe once more in expressing her dependence on him. Mercanton shrugged her hand away and shifted in his chair.

"You understand the situation," Chandler continued. "If we re-establish contact, you will go on exactly as before. Only, we will supply your information and we'll hope to get valuable information out of the Germans. If you fail to make contact, well—we'll see." He tried to make his last words sound as ominous as possible. If this morning's failure had been faked by Mercanton in an effort to extricate himself from the affair, he surely wouldn't repeat his mistake now.

"I know you can have complete confidence that my husband will do everything he possibly can," Marthe said with conviction.

"I hope so," said Chandler coolly. He would have to go slowly. He couldn't allow himself to slide into a friendly acceptance of these people. He assumed an authoritative manner. "Now then. I think we'd better settle on some story that will explain my being here."

"That won't be difficult," said Marthe. "We've been here a very short time ourselves. We know very few people here."

"Good. Well, then, let's say I'm a member of your family. I've been wounded in the Resistance and I've been invalided out."

"Better say a friend of the family," said Marthe, interest brightening her voice. "You've been sent to us by a member of our family. That will make more sense to the children and it won't matter if we don't know very much about each other."

"Good. Well then. My name is Roger Dulin and I was born in a suburb of Paris."

"I noticed you have the accent of Paris," said Marthe with a hint of playfulness. "Does your wound bother you much?"

"No. It's an injury to my back." Roger smiled in spite of himself. "It just makes it impossible for me to do any more fighting."

"That's a very good sort of wound to have," said Marthe. She laughed shyly, a light warm laugh. Chandler felt an instant response stir in him. He looked across at her and laughed too. Mercanton sat watching closely, a faint smile on his lips, tentative plans and conjectures crowding his mind.

II

After instructing Mercanton not to leave the property, Chandler excused himself to take a nap. Marthe showed him to a small room in the wing over the utility rooms. Like the rest of the house, it was simple and agreeable, with whitewashed walls, rusty linen curtains at the windows, and a wide inviting wooden bed. He had brought a few extra shirts and a toilet-kit with him, and these he put neatly away in the bureau. He locked the radio in the closet and put a hair in the lock so that he would know if it were tampered with. As soon as he heard Marthe return to the ground floor, he went out and tiptoed quickly up to the attic. He was going to search the whole house, but he wished to do it without the occupants' knowledge so that they wouldn't be put on their guard.

In the attic, he found trunks full of old clothes, some

odds and ends of furniture, several big bundles of family photographs and old books. He worked quickly and silently. He was careful to leave everything as he found it. From time to time he glanced out the window. He could see the children leaping about on the nearby terraces, a foolish little snapping dog at their heels. Mercanton was hammering in the courtyard below, reconditioning a dilapidated wheelbarrow. Marthe came and went, tending her chickens, gathering herbs, calling warnings to the children. The sun was blazing now, destroying perspective and staring down the exuberant colors of the countryside.

Once, glancing out the window, Chandler saw Marthe approach Mercanton. She stood close to him as he bent over the barrow, speaking in a subdued voice as if she felt she were being watched. Her words rose barely audible to Chandler.

"Shouldn't you rest, dear one?" she asked gently. Chandler could hear only a mutter from Mercanton as he continued to concentrate on the barrow.

"But your face," Marthe insisted. "What have they done to your face?" Chandler could see the muscles in Mercanton's back tense before he straightened himself and turned towards Marthe. He paused a moment before replying.

"Oh, that? It's nothing. Just a misunderstanding." His fingers gingerly touched one of the bruises on his face as he spoke. Marthe darted a quick glance towards the house.

"You must remember, the Americans are not like us," she said. "You must try to understand them."

"The Americans are barbarians. They will apologize before we're through." Mercanton's guarded exterior seemed to give way under a burst of anger.

"No. You mustn't say that," Marthe said, lowering her voice still more. She placed a placating hand on his arm. "What did they do to you?"

"Nothing at all," he said, remembering himself. He went on, trying to achieve a note of hauteur which wavered unconvincingly into a kind of desperate self-assertion: "They want me to work with them. You heard it yourself. We talked it all over and they asked me to work with them. I agreed. They thought they had to frighten me into it, but of course, I was glad to work with them."

"Of course," Marthe agreed soothingly. "I don't understand all this, but I'm sure everything will be all right. At least, you are here."

"Certainly, I'm here. What did you expect?"

"Nothing. But last night I was frightened. I'm glad you're here. And this young man seems sympathetic. I'm sure everything will work out all right."

"Everything will be all right. I told you that." Mercanton turned back to the barrow, as if dismissing the subject. Marthe hesitated, looking down on him, then turned and walked back towards the vineyard.

Chandler left the window and began to repack the last trunk he had opened. What a nasty mess. The poor guy probably did think that everything would be all right. He must do everything in his power to increase that feeling of confidence, make Mercanton forget the humiliation he had received at the hands of the Americans. Mercanton must never be allowed to believe that there was anything to be gained by betraying the game to the Germans. He must be wooed and won and presented, ardently pro-Allied, to the firing squad. Of course, there was still the possibility that the radio contact wouldn't be successful.

So they had found him sympathetic. That was a step in the right direction. He wondered what they would think of him should they find him searching furtively through their belongings. It was fantastic. He had always believed that it was almost criminal to read somebody else's mail. This was infinitely worse. But it was sort of interesting, really. Strange how easily social taboos gave way to basic impulses. Like this rather cheap curiosity about the private accumulations of other people's lives.

He closed the lid of the trunk and looked around once more to be sure that he was leaving everything in order. He left the attic and went down to the second floor where he started with the Mercantons' bedroom. He found nothing but rows of dresses and suits, drawers full of linens, underclothes and toilet articles. He was embarrassed by the intimate odor of daily living. Two small rooms were set aside for the children—a grubby confusion of clothes and dolls and tin soldiers, and a drawer full of rather soiled stones which Chandler presumed to be a mineralogical collection. There were also rows of textbooks and exercise books, and Chandler learned that the younger boy, Pierre, was a model student.

Beyond his own room, Chandler found a linen room and another spare bedroom which was dominated by an absurdly antiquated sewing machine. There was nothing here but the carefully sorted overflow of any well-run household. It was just a little after noon when Chandler made his way back to his own room and lay down on the bed to await a call to luncheon. When it came, he found

that he was to eat alone. Mercanton was waiting for him
when he came down to the dining room.

"I think I'll have a siesta myself, if that's agreeable to
you," he said.

"Yes, of course. Go right ahead," said Chandler. "Have
you all eaten?"

"Yes. My wife thought you'd prefer it."

"I didn't want to disturb you," said Marthe, entering
from the kitchen. She spoke with the solicitous humility
of a well-bred housekeeper. "Did you sleep well?"

"Fine, thanks. But from now on, I'd like to eat with the
rest of you. You shouldn't have taken this trouble."

"Just as you wish," Marthe said with unyielding formal-
ity. "What time do you like to have your meals?"

"Whenever you're used to having them," said Roger.
He felt intensely uncomfortable. It was so difficult to hit
the right note in his relations with these people. He must
invite their friendship, yet he must hold himself apart,
eternally watchful. He must learn his lines, like an actor,
so that they'd come out smoothly even when he was thinking of something else. Yet all his life he had struggled to
free himself from the emptiness of false dealings with
people. It did something to you. You got so you couldn't
tell what was real. Like his mother effusively greeting
someone he knew she detested.

Above all, he couldn't bear being treated with deference.
He had always been surrounded by people who deferred
to his family's position. It had always seemed to set a limit
on his individuality. He went on:

"Look, I'd like you to think of me as a sort of guest here.

You know, a part of the family. I don't want you to take any trouble over me."

"That's very kind of you," said Mercanton. He exchanged a look with Marthe. He was willing enough to establish an atmosphere of mutual understanding. He wished to explore every aspect of this young man whom he regarded instinctively as his adversary. But he had permitted himself little experience of intimate relationships. He wasn't sure how to start. "We hope you'll be comfortable here," he added, experimentally.

"Sure. I like it here," said Chandler.

"Well, see you later."

"Good. See you later." Chandler listened to Mercanton mount the stairs. Pretty good guy, he thought, not for the first time that day. The whole thing was funny, in a way. This is it, he said to himself, flexing his jaw muscles. Captain Chandler goes gallantly into action. In a sun-drenched vineyard surrounded by goats and chickens and rabbits. Captain Chandler, armed only with a false identity card, outwits a desperate gang of three French school children. Captain Chandler, hero of the barnyard offensive. Oh brother, what a war.

Marthe served him an excellent lunch of poached eggs, a green salad, cheese and fruit, accompanied by a good harsh red wine.

"This is good," said Roger. "You have no trouble getting food here?"

"Oh, it's not easy," said Marthe. Her tone was more natural now. Chandler noticed that she seemed to relax when she wasn't aware of Mercanton—or when he was out of the room. "We're lucky here. All this is right from the place, except the cheese. I traded a pair of evening slippers for the cheese. Heaven knows why anybody wants evening slippers now."

"When I go back to Marseille, I'll try to bring you some of our Army rations."

"That would be wonderful," Marthe said doubtfully. "I understand all your food is powdered."

"Powdered?"

"Yes. I know some people who bought eggs and milk and coffee from an American soldier. It was all powder."

"Oh, yes. Well, we have a lot of powdered things," Roger said, definitely conscious of the woman's charm. "But we have regular food too."

"It must be very interesting to eat everything powdered," said Marthe with droll irony.

After lunch, Marthe followed her husband upstairs for a siesta. Left alone, Chandler crossed the foyer into the living room. Here the blinds on the windows, and on the long French doors that opened onto the terrace, were closed against the blinding midday sun. It was cool and dark. It was so quiet in the house that he could hear the paper of his cigarette burn as he took a deep puff. The room was more elaborately furnished than the rest of the house. There were a couple of ornate pieces of Louis Seize furniture, a mirror in a heavy gilt frame, several delicate chairs upholstered in faded silk. It had an unlived-in air.

He went directly to the secretary standing against the wall and continued his search. He found several drawers locked, which he opened quickly with two bits of stiff wire he carried in his pocket. There were masses of accounts, old letters, receipted bills. Under one pile of papers he found a loaded thirty-two caliber revolver which he emptied and replaced. There were copies of a lengthy correspondence with the Vichy government, which simply substantiated the story Mercanton had already told, and a copy of a long letter addressed to Pierre Laval, setting forth Mercanton's considerable achievements and his unfaltering devotion to the Maréchal. Chandler slipped several of these letters into his pocket, not because they shed any new light on the case, but because they might prove valuable as evidence in case Mercanton ever came before a tribunal. There was nothing else of interest.

When he was finished, Chandler's attention was caught by a small framed photograph on the top of the desk. It showed Mercanton in uniform when he couldn't have been much more than twenty. There was a callow roughness in the face that suggested his provincial background. It lacked the urbane assurance that characterized Mercanton today. But there was an eager intentness of expression that was arresting. Chandler had seen that look on the faces of some of the boys he had gone to school and college with—restless, absorbed, unapproachable. They were young men dedicated to careers, whether through inclination or the press of environmental influence. Their blinding ambition cut them off from a life of varied experiences. They led cramped, withdrawn lives, looking towards something beyond. He had always respected them, even though he felt sorry for them, and had gone out of his way to make friends with them. Yes, this young Mercanton was someone he knew. The feeling of recognition was strong in him. The years stood aside and, briefly, something of the motivating essence of this unhappy man was illuminated.

Another wave of distaste for his job came over him, and he pushed the papers back in the drawer and turned the locks with the two pieces of strong wire. He got up and went to the kitchen. There, he went through the orderly cupboards, even looking into the pots. He had no idea what he was looking for so he had to look everywhere. He was glad to find that there was no back stairway. It made it easier to check the movements of the family. From the kitchen, he went back to the front of the house and out through the courtyard to the other wing. Here the search got out of hand. In the confusion of chicken roosts, racked wine bottles, bales of straw, rabbit pens and old tools, almost anything could be concealed. Chandler went through it all as thoroughly as possible. He was now at least familiar with the lay of the house.

III

LATE in the afternoon, Roger was still poking about when he heard the children tumbling out of the house and racing off into the vineyard. He gave them a few moments to clear off and then he walked back to the living quarters. He found Marthe and Mercanton just emerging from their nap.

"Wouldn't you like to look around the place?" Marthe inquired. She was wearing a bright-patterned peasant dress which contrasted piquantly with her clever caricature of a face. Her red-brown hair was bound up tightly in a kerchief.

"Sure. I'd like to," said Chandler. "I've been looking around a little this afternoon."

"But you must meet the animals. The animals are the most important things here." They went out into the courtyard. It was cooling off now. The sun was low over the near hills. The shadows were deepening around the house. In its baroque font the spring was bubbling restfully.

"This is my favorite time of day," said Marthe. Care had gone from her face. She seemed almost light-hearted.

Roger looked about him and his heart was suddenly constricted by the graceful delicacy of the landscape. A light breeze was rippling through the olive trees, turning them from silver to grey green. The mellow lemon walls of the house glowed through the shadow of the great oaks. Peace lay in the air like a tender memory. Christ, this damn war, thought Chandler. His throat felt tight and dry.

Over by the door of their roost, the flock of chickens were scratching for food, bobbing in their precise little minuet like mechanical toys.

"The chickens are mine," said Marthe. "They all have names. The children have given them all the names of flowers. I think they got the idea because of the name of the house. This one is Jasmin. The little white one there is Serpolet. Mimosa is my favorite—the yellow one."

"How can you possibly tell the difference between one chicken and another?" asked Roger.

"Have you never known any chickens? They're all very different. You should study them. They're very interesting."

"Come see the rabbits," said Mercanton, impatiently.

"Oh, you must admire his rabbits," Marthe said. "My husband thinks his rabbits are the most remarkable rabbits in the world."

"No, I don't," Mercantan said seriously. "But they're very good rabbits." They went in to where the rabbits, in all sizes and colors, were ranged in cages.

"What do you keep them for? Do you eat them?" Roger asked.

"Oh yes, we eat them," said Marthe. "We grow very attached to them but we eat them. We try to eat the least attractive ones first."

"You have an awful lot of them," said Roger, smiling.

"They have so many babies," Marthe explained.

"It's very curious," said Mercanton, bewilderment in his face. "I keep the males locked up by themselves, but they have babies anyway."

"I think he has more to learn of rabbit anatomy," said Marthe. She caught Roger's eye and they both burst into laughter.

They were still discussing the ingenuity of the rabbits when they heard the voices of the children outside. They went out and found them entering the courtyard with three goats. The procession was led by the eight-year-old, Pierre, sitting astride a big white goat, like an illustration for an ancient myth. Dominique, the elder boy, led the other two goats, with four-year-old Françoise walking at his side. The same snapping little dog Roger had noticed earlier ran importantly back and forth, pretending that the goats were its particular responsibility. As Roger and the Mercantons watched, Pierre turned aside and rode grandly in through the front door of the house.

"Pay no attention to that," Marthe said. "He likes to ride around the dining room table. Dominique, come here and meet our guest."

Dominique came forward and shook hands solemnly with Chandler, then pushed Françoise forward paternally to make a formal little bob. Chandler thought the boy seemed nervous and reserved. He strongly resembled his father. In a moment, Pierre emerged from the house, still superbly mounted on the goat. He rode majestically over to the others, dismounted, pushed his hair back shyly from his forehead and, beaming irresistibly, shook hands with the stranger.

"And this is Pensée," said Marthe, indicating the agitated little dog, who instantly drew back and bared its teeth. "Poor Pensée. She is really neuter. She's neither a boy nor a girl. Something went wrong somewhere. It makes her unhappy." They all wandered slowly back towards the house, chatting agreeably, pausing to attend to the day's final chores as they went.

They ate dinner that evening on the terrace under a roof of trailing vines. It was agreed that the fiction of Dulin should be expanded to include an extended stay in the United States so that they could talk freely of America in front of the children. Marthe served another excellent meal of soup, civet of rabbit, a casserole of tomatoes and eggplant, and fruit. She regarded Roger with apprehension as he helped himself to each dish.

"You can eat all these things?" she inquired finally.

"Sure. Why not? It's all wonderful."

"I didn't know. They eat such strange things in America. I remember we went once to an American restaurant in Paris, and there was whipped cream on the salad. You remember, Jean Louis?"

"Indeed I do. I remember, too, they served jam with the ham. It was odd."

"You could possibly get used to such things," said Marthe without conviction.

"I suppose you could." Roger laughed. "I'd rather not, though."

"I found a dead man this afternoon," said little Pierre suddenly, beaming happily.

"You found what?" asked Mercanton severely. The child held the attention of the entire table. He looked around, smiling proudly, pleased with his conversational gambit. "A dead man," he said. "He smelled."

"Pierre!" exclaimed Marthe. "You must forgive him, M. Dulin."

"Where did you find this dead man?" demanded Mercanton.

"Up in the woods behind the vineyard. It was a Boche."

"Good Heavens, he must have been there for over a week," Mercanton said.

"Poor creature. Isn't it terrible?" said Marthe, genuinely shocked.

"He didn't have very much face," added Pierre brightly, sensing that the conversation was getting out of his control.

"That's enough, Pierre," Marthe said. "Jean Louis, you must notify the authorities first thing in the morning."

"Did you have much fighting around here?" Roger asked.

"Not very much," said Mercanton. "A few Germans

stayed behind to try to block the road. For a few days we heard firing quite close, but we all stayed in the house."

"You can have no idea what it was like," said Marthe. "When we heard that the Americans had landed on the coast, it was like waking up after a bad dream. We had lived in the shadows for four years."

"But you believed in Pétain?"

"Yes. At first, he was like a standard. When we heard him talking to us on the radio he gave us hope when we thought everything was over. Today, everybody will tell you that they always hated the Maréchal. But it's not true. At first, most people believed in him. He was a symbol. Later, people began to learn things. But you know, we've had very little news all these years. We heard things very slowly. And then . . ." Marthe faltered. She finished slowly: "And then, for many people it was too late." In her eyes was great sorrow, and a plea for understanding. Roger looked quickly at Mercanton. He wasn't sure he would be able to meet his eyes. But Mercanton was sitting motionless, his head averted.

Roger pushed his chair back from the table. He wasn't hungry any more. Silence fell over the little group. Even the children seemed to feel the agony enclose them. The lingering dusk had finally given way to night and the stars had taken possession of the sky. Nearby, a nightingale sang its infinitely varied and heartbreaking song.

They all went to bed early that night. Just as they were preparing to go upstairs, Mercanton drew Chandler into the living room.

"There is something I want to speak to you about," he

said. He hesitated and Chandler felt obliged to encourage him to continue.

"Go ahead," Chandler said. "I want you to speak to me about anything that comes into your mind. We'll be able to work together much better that way."

"Well, it's really my wife's idea," said Mercanton. "You see, she feels that perhaps we aren't safe. I have a gun here. She wants me to keep it with me. But I didn't want to touch it without speaking to you about it first."

"Yes, of course." Chandler was thinking rapidly. This wasn't the move of a conspirator. It was, indeed, disarmingly straightforward. But how was he to tell the Frenchman not to carry the gun without making him feel like a prisoner? He hurried on smoothly: "I don't think you need worry. I am armed. And if we should run into any sort of difficulty, I wouldn't want you to be involved. The most important thing is for you not to get mixed up with the authorities in any way. Your work is too important." Rather neat, Chandler thought. With practice, he would be quite good at this.

"I understand," Mercanton said approvingly. "I'll explain that to my wife." They went out and Marthe joined them. The French couple escorted Roger to the door of his room. They shook hands with him and wished him good night, then Marthe left him with Mercanton.

"Until tomorrow morning," said Mercanton, trying to sound confident. "I hope everything goes well tomorrow morning."

"I hope so too. I'm sure it will."

"But if it doesn't?" Mercanton asked, his voice pale with concern.

Roger felt an impulse to say something reassuring. But it was too soon to remove the threat of retribution from the man's mind. The situation was not yet clear. He couldn't permit himself to believe in the man's sincerity. And what if contact weren't reestablished? Roger thought of the dispatch with which other captured agents had been disposed of.

"Well," he said, trying not to sound too cold, "there's no point thinking about that." They wished each other good night once more and Roger entered his room.

He closed the door and stood behind it, listening. He heard the couple preparing for bed, crossing the hall into the bathroom, exchanging snatches of trivial conversation. At last, the house was quiet. Roger slipped off his shoes, crossed over to the bureau and took out his toilet kit. He found a bottle of Benzedrine and took two tablets, leaning his head far back and dropping them into the back of his throat. He picked up a blanket from the foot of the bed and went out into the hall. He stopped in front of the Mercantons' room for a moment and listened. He could hear the faint sound for regular breathing and, once, the rustling of sheets and the creak of a bed. He turned and went downstairs to the living room. In the dark, he pulled the most comfortable chair over to the door, just off the foyer, where he could watch the stairs. He sat down, placed his automatic on the floor beside him, and wrapped the blanket around his legs. There he would remain until morning. If Mercanton had any plans for the night, he would know about them. He sincerely hoped his host would stay sensibly in his bed.

IV

ROGER was nervous and wide-awake. The Benzedrine was
working in him, making him light-headed and ill-tempered.
Thoughts crowded through his mind, claiming attention
for a moment, then dropping out of his consciousness. He
went through the events of the last two days once more,
searching for some new angle, some forgotten clue. For a
moment, he thought of Meddling. God, what a bastard!
He was surprised at the vigor with which he had grown
to dislike him in the last twenty-four hours. He found himself thinking of ways in which he might avoid further
contact with him.

His mind went blank, and then began poking about in
odd corners of his consciousness, looking for something
to hold on to. He wondered what people would be doing
in New York. Just finishing work probably and heading
home for a cocktail before dinner. Or were the late spots
just urging the last customers out the door to pick their
way home past the men hosing the pavements in the grey
light of early dawn? He never could get this time business
straight. He tried to concentrate, making his hands into
the sun and earth, and passing them back and forth around
each other. No. It was no use. He would have to leave
the universe to its own devices.

He wondered what his family would think of him now
if they could see him sitting with a gun at his feet, playing
jailer to a Nazi spy. They would probably think it was
not quite nice. They had a comfortable way of closing
their eyes to anything unpleasant or unfamiliar in life. They
had a profound conviction of the rectitude of their own

attitudes, their own way of life. They were incapable of understanding anything that might shake that conviction. He thought of his family fondly, but with little real feeling. There had never been a close family relationship. They had always lived in a comfortable house in East Sixty-fifth Street. His mother and father had been busy with their own lives. He and his younger brother had spent most of their childhood away at school. As soon as he was old enough, his holidays had been spent at parties in New York and in traveling abroad with friends.

He smiled to himself as he thought of the shocked concern with which his father had learned of his participation in the strike at Yale. He treated it as he might have treated news that his son had taken up with a chorus girl. "I was quite a radical myself when I was a youngster," he had said in a hearty man-to-man manner. "Nothing wrong with that sort of thing if you don't take it too seriously. Of course, a lot of people might not understand. You don't want to get yourself known as a crackpot." Roger chuckled soundlessly in the dark. His father was all right. Just a little old-fashioned.

The image of the girl he was unofficially engaged to filled his mind, and for an instant he remembered her warmly, the way her hair fell softly around her shoulders, the tenderness in her eyes, the young excitement of her body. Christ, he wished he'd been to bed with her. But it had seemed wrong, somehow. Her name was Carol Houston. He had known her all his life. She was the sort of girl his family approved of—the right background and all that. But she understood a lot of things, too. He could talk to her. The memory of her set his mind working towards the future. For months, all through his training, he had been able to think only of the job he was being prepared for. His mind couldn't go beyond it. Now that the textbook problems had become flesh and blood reality, he was freed from the present. He could look into the future. In a way, it was as if the future were over for him. He could begin to think, for the first time in his life really, of a career, a home, of whatever it was that went with a normal, peaceful existence. The future would surely include Carol. But he was going to take things easy at first. Look around. He wasn't going to get caught in the life that would have been laid out for him by his family. He wanted to see the country. He might settle in some new place and get a job on a newspaper. And go into politics, maybe. He must find time to write to Carol soon and start making plans.

Time was observing its endless, irregular progress, marked by the chimes of the big clock in the living room. Sometimes, such a long period elapsed between the striking of the clock that Roger thought it must have stopped. At other times the hours followed themselves in such rapid succession that he was afraid he might have slept. At last he noticed the faint outlines of the room emerging from the lifting darkness. A few minutes before six, he pushed the chair back into place and returned to his room. He was just in time. As he stretched himself out on his bed, he heard the first stirrings of the family.

V

Shortly after six, Mercanton knocked on his door to wake him. He took the radio out of the closet and went up to the attic. Mercanton joined him there. In the time left before the scheduled transmission, Mercanton carefully checked his set.

"Everything all right?" Roger asked.

"Yes, everything seems to be all right." Mercanton repeated the routine of the previous morning, starting promptly at six-thirty. Roger stood by the window, watching and listening. As before, he saw Mercanton's body gather in intense concentration as time passed with no results. It looked as if this were going to be another fruitless effort. Too bad, Roger thought. They would try a few more times and then he would have to take Mercanton back to Marseille and a quick death. Maybe it would be better that way. It would save them all the pain of a lingering deception. Mercanton was oblivious of the young man watching him. His strained energies were directed at the machine in front of him. He felt cornered and betrayed. Mother of God, what was the matter with the idiots? They had never failed to make contact before. He wondered if he dared fake a contact. It would be difficult. He would have to plan it carefully. The American knew too much about radio. He twisted the dial savagely. Finally, he snapped off the current and sat motionless, staring in front of him. His whole body felt blunted.

"Well, there you are," he said.

"Yes, it's curious," said Roger bleakly. He turned and looked out the window, wondering what his next move should be. He was just swinging back to face Mercanton, when he caught a flicker of movement out of the corner of his eye and his attention froze. From where he stood, he could see part of a small abandoned shed just off the drive down near the gate. As he watched, a head emerged from the door of the shed, looked about cautiously, and then a young man stepped out onto the drive. Roger caught only a fleeting glimpse of spectacles, rough country clothes, and what appeared to be heavy military boots, before he flung himself at the door.

"Bring the radio down," he said as he ran past Mercanton. He was down the stairs, out of the house and running down the drive within a few seconds. He ran straight to the gate, glancing into the empty shed as he passed it, and out onto the lane. He looked up and down. There was nobody in sight. He cut back through the gate and leaped into the terraced vineyard, doubling back and forth between the rows. It was broken terrain offering easy concealment. After a few moments he pulled himself up, breathing hard. He realized that he was too late. He walked down through the terraces back to the shed. It was empty except for a broken plow and a pile of weathered straw. He leaned over and turned up some of the straw. His hand brushed against a bit of crumpled paper. He picked it out and looked at it. It was an empty package of cigarettes, bearing a German trademark. He stood turning it over in his hands for almost a minute. Then he smoothed it out carefully, folded it and put it in his pocket. He left the shed and walked back to the house, thoughtfully humming an improvised tune.

CHAPTER

Five

I

MARTHE and Jean Louis Mercanton were standing in the door when Roger entered the courtyard.

"Is anything wrong?" Mercanton inquired uneasily.

Roger hesitated. All his suspicions were aroused. He was not going to be taken in by this couple. They were persuasive, appealing, but maybe they were up to something. There must be some connection between Mercanton and the figure he had glimpsed at the shed. Perhaps Mercanton was keeping in touch with his German masters through this outside contact. For an instant, Roger played with the idea of saying nothing about the incident. He could wait and see if Mercanton would reveal himself. It might be more effective to catch him red-handed. No. He'd better take no chances—he would pretend to know more than he did and try to trick Mercanton into a confession.

"Will you please come inside?" said Roger. He walked past the couple and led the way into the living room. He waited until they had entered the room, then closed the door. They stood facing him gravely, expectantly.

89

"I just saw him," Roger said, meaningfully.

"You saw him? What do you mean?" Mercanton asked.

Roger took the cigarette package from his pocket, unfolded it and held it out to Mercanton. Mercanton didn't touch it, but studied it as it lay in Roger's hand. He looked up, puzzled.

"I know the brand," he said. "It's the brand distributed to the German Army. Where did you find it?"

"In the shed down by the gate. You know the man who left it." Roger spoke as if making a statement of fact. Marthe took a quick, sharp breath.

"I know the man? I don't understand. Who left it?" Mercanton demanded.

"You know of nobody who's been here for the last two days?" It was less a question than a stern reminder.

"But nobody's been here for the last two days. Or longer. That's true, isn't it, dear?" He turned to Marthe, who stood beside him listening attentively.

"Yes, that's true," she said. "But don't you understand? He means, they're trying to do you harm. Isn't that it?" She turned to Roger. "You think they've left somebody here to do him harm?"

"You needn't worry about that," Roger said, with some annoyance. She was turning him aside from his purpose, appealing to him as an ally. It made his methods seem crude and presumptuous.

"I've been afraid of it ever since I knew what my husband was doing. I know that if ever anything goes wrong, they'll try to punish him." She spoke calmly, as if stating an obvious truth. Roger felt himself thrown off balance once more.

"You're sure you've seen nobody hanging around the place recently?" he asked, his tone softening.

"We'd have told you if we had," said Mercanton. "What's happened?"

Roger paused to reconsider his ground. His little ruse had failed. But he couldn't believe the couple was deceiving him. They assumed that Roger accepted them on their own terms. It was a kind of proof of innocence. If they had anything to hide, they would be more plausible. They would make an effort to concoct explanations that would lull his suspicions. All the same, the puzzle of the stranger in the shed remained unsolved. Possibly if he told them everything, they could arrive at an explanation together. He found himself telling them what he'd just seen from the window upstairs.

"I understand now why you're worried," Marthe said when he had finished. "The night Jean Louis. . . . The night my husband was with you I heard Pensée barking several times near the gate. I slept very little that night. I got up once but I couldn't see anything. Otherwise, I've noticed nothing unusual, but I've been frightened. You can understand that. You think somebody has been staying in the shed, watching the house? I tell you, if they find out what my husband is doing, they'll try to kill him."

"Your husband will be safe as long as he's working with us," said Roger. Mercanton spread his hands and clicked his tongue impatiently at his wife, as if to say, "What did I tell you?"

Roger went on firmly: "But let me tell you this. We have ways of getting information from Germany. We even have ways of finding out how you stand with the

Germans. It takes time, but eventually we can find out. So if you do anything that tips them off that you're working with us, we'll find out about it. It'll be better for you if you tell me everything that might have some connection with this business. Even if you make some slip, or remember something you should have told us earlier, it'll be better if you're completely frank with me. Everything, you understand. The smallest details."

"Certainly, monsieur," said Mercanton. "But that's extraordinary. You can really get such information out of Germany still? You must have a formidable service." His voice was firm with genuine admiration.

"It's pretty thorough . . ." Roger checked himself abruptly. The high, nervous yapping of the little dog rose from the direction of the drive. The three of them stood motionless for an instant, looking into each other's eyes. Then Roger stepped quickly through the French doors onto the terrace and hurried down the drive. The little dog was down near the gate, running about in agitated circles, barking furiously. There was nobody in sight.

II

LATER in the day, Roger drove Mercanton into Aix. Its fine, wide old main street lay peaceful and inviting in the mottled shade of the great plane trees. The simple eighteenth-century doorways seemed to chill with their elegance the bright rude sun. Roger parked his car in front of the Café des Deux Hommes. There were a handful of American soldiers sprawled possessively around its ugly wicker sidewalk tables. As he passed, they looked at him and made some outspoken remarks about the lousy French bastards who didn't fight their own war. Several doors down, a couple of villainous-looking Frenchmen, rigged out in an imaginative array of British and American military equipment, stood desultory guard in front of the headquarters of the Resistance. Roger accompanied Mercanton while he reported the presence of the German corpse on his property. He was gratified to observe the courtesy with which Mercanton was received. For here was another possible source of danger. The men of the Resistance wasted no polite words on those suspected of having dealt with Vichy. Roger hoped he would be spared the necessity of protecting Mercanton from his own countrymen.

When the corpse was properly registered, Roger left Mercanton in the car and went to establish the procedure that was to become routine in the weeks that followed. He walked down the street until he found a well-frequented cafe where he wouldn't be noticed. He went in and put in a call to Marseille.

"This is Dulin," he said to the Frenchman who answered the phone. He chatted aimlessly for several minutes about imaginary family and friends. "Everything's fine here. I hope to see you soon," he said at last and rung off. He had decided not to mention the episode of the shed. It wouldn't be possible to report the thing in detail over the phone, and Meddling might take alarm and call the whole plan off. Nothing would be gained by that. He might as well give Mercanton a chance to prove himself. He would tell Meddling about the unknown visitor when he knew more about him. Or when the other circumstances of the case had clarified themselves.

III

THAT night, Roger continued his solitary vigil. But now there was a difference. His watch no longer had to be kept a secret from the Mercantons. The possibility that danger lay outside made it a reasonable precaution. The fact that they were aware of him sitting awake in the night relieved his sense of isolation. Already a change was taking place in their relationship. Without realizing it, he had become their guardian, not their keeper.

He made several stealthy trips down to the shed by the gate, but each time he found it empty. His nerves were stretched taut by lack of sleep and the increased doses of Benzedrine. The hours dragged intolerably and he jumped slightly every time the big clock struck. He felt giddy and his head ached dully. He sat tensed, his mind a blank resistance, his curious fingers hooked cruelly around the arms of the chair, listening for a sound that never came.

Two more days passed. Each morning, Roger and Mercanton made their futile search of the airwaves. They spent one afternoon taking the radio apart and checking all its mechanism. Roger snatched an hour or two of sleep when he could, but mostly he lived on his nerves and Benzedrine. He kept a close watch on the shed, but he never found anything. He made his phone call to Marseille regularly. Gloom and a nervous alarm settled into the house like an unwanted guest. None of them could avoid it. It gave to the shining days a baffling unreality. At first, they tried to exorcise the presence with spirited talk, but everything seemed to lead inevitably to the question in all their minds, and soon they settled into an uneasy silence.

They were all keeping watch on each other, observing each other secretly, waiting for a break in the other's guard. Roger was puzzled by the failure of radio contact, alternately considering and rejecting any number of sinister explanations. He was careful to draw back whenever he felt himself slipping into familiarity with the family. He watched every move each member made, ready to act at the first damning revelation.

Mercanton, too, had a cautious feeling that he must prepare himself in some way. Harried by the certain fate that awaited him should he fail to reestablish contact, he allowed himself to explore wild and impossible schemes for his own liberation. He might even be able to dispose of this young American. If he could have thought of some way to ensure the safety of his family, he might have done it. He had nothing to lose. Marthe sensed her husband's dangerous mood and tried to steady him. She felt increasingly the sympathy in Roger, and knew they could count on him, if only . . . if only. . . . It was the way all their thoughts ended.

Aware that something was wrong, the children slipped quietly in and out of the house, going about their chores on the place. Sometimes Marthe would embark on a gay little song, but after the first few notes her voice would trail away and the house would be given back to the prowling distrust.

I V

ON THE morning of the fifth day, barely halfway through the scheduled ordeal with the radio, Mercanton seized the receiving unit of the set, wrenched it from its place and looked at it angrily. His fingers poked viciously about among its intricate parts and he slammed it back into its case. Roger moved forward quickly.

"Take it easy," he said. "It's not going to do any good breaking it." But Mercanton wasn't listening. His shoulders were back, his face had cleared.

"There it is," he said. "I've got it!"

Roger put his head down close to Mercanton's earphones. Clear and thin, forcing its way through the static and interference, came the call from Germany. "RLM" it insisted over and over again, like the voice of a lost child. Roger felt a tremor run down his spine. His heart was beating fast.

"For God's sake, answer it," he said. "Don't let it get away."

Mercanton made a confident gesture. Satisfaction lit his face. He sat listening for a few more seconds, then cut in with his own call. His hands moved with assurance. He was relaxed and adroit. Roger stood behind him, admiring his expertness. The preliminaries over, Mercanton began taking a message, a scramble of letters in bizarre sequence. He worked rapidly, interrupting occasionally to ask for a repeat. When it was finished, he verified its length and checked its date on one of the charts hanging on the wall in front of him. "OK," Mercanton signalled, and Roger listened while the German operator beat out the rhythm of the classic Americanism, "Shave and a haircut." "Six bits," added Mercanton on his key. He snapped off the radio and stood up. He was laughing a little breathlessly, like a man who has just won a race.

"There you are," he said. "I knew we'd get somewhere if we kept trying."

"Sure. Now we're getting somewhere." Unaccountably, Roger shared Mercanton's sense of triumph. He put his hand on the Frenchman's shoulder. "What in the world did you do to the radio?"

"Nothing. I just shook it." He laughed again, appealingly, like a boy.

"And it began to operate, just like that?"

"Just like that. It's what they call the imponderable in radio."

"Well, let's go see what our friends have to say." They went downstairs laughing and chatting, pausing while Roger locked up the radio. Marthe was waiting for them at the foot of the stairs, as was her custom.

"Good morning," she said. "Everything is all right?"

"Yes. Everything's fine," Roger replied.

"I'm very glad." She looked at her husband a long moment, her eyes shining radiantly, then hurried to the kitchen.

Roger went into the living room, laid out paper and began decoding the message. Mercanton sat beside him, offering suggestions. While he worked, Roger could hear the children outside calling to each other. In the kitchen, Marthe was singing. Relief was flowing into the house like a transfusion.

As the message began to emerge into the clear, Roger worked more and more clumsily. His hands were shaking perceptibly, and as each word formed itself, his mind raced ahead to guess the full import of the message. At last it was finished: WHAT'S GOING ON. QUESTION. HAVE HEARD

YOU EVERY DAY BUT YOU FAIL TO RESPOND TO CALL. SHOULD WE CHANGE FREQUENCY. QUESTION. INFORMED AMERICAN THIRTY FOURTH DIVISION DUE SHORTLY MARSEILLE. PLEASE OBTAIN NUMBER OF TROOPS, INSIGNIA, TYPE OF ARMS AND EQUIPMENT, NAMES OF COMMANDERS, DESTINATION. REALIZE THIS IS A LOT TO ASK BUT DO YOUR BEST. BE CAREFUL. REGARDS. BLUM.

Roger took a deep breath and handed the paper over to Mercanton. "Who's Blum?" he asked. "What do you know about him?"

"I know nothing," Mercanton said. "That's the way the messages are always signed." He read through the message quickly and glanced up at Roger, a faint smile on his lips. "You see, they have lots of confidence in me."

"Yes. It looks all right," said Roger, studying the paper once more. "Tell me. Suppose I weren't here. How would you go about answering these questions?"

"I haven't the slightest idea. This is the first time they've asked such things."

"But you surely knew this is the sort of thing they'd want to know."

"I don't know. I never really thought about it. How *do* you get such information?"

Roger laughed, a sudden, happy laugh. Mercanton seemed so genuinely helpless under these circumstances. "It shouldn't even be possible. I can tell you that," he said.

"But it's very important, don't you think?" asked Mercanton earnestly. "We must be very careful how we answer these questions."

"Yes, of course. Very careful. I'll go into Marseille later."

"Would you like to have breakfast now?" Mercanton inquired.

"Sure. Let's have breakfast." Roger folded the final draft of the message and put it in his pocket. He gathered up the papers on which he had been working, placed them in a large ash tray and set fire to them. The two men stood watching the small flame.

"You are satisfied with everything now?" Mercanton asked. He saw the flame spurt up as it took hold of the last crumpled corner of the paper. All his fears seemed to be burned out of him, too. Not that he had been exactly afraid. He never doubted that he would reestablish contact. He was an experienced radio operator. Still, it had been unpleasant. Now he could settle down to work. He was willing to forget the incident at the Marseille head-quarters. The Americans hadn't realized what sort of man they were dealing with. They must accept him now as a full partner.

"Yes. I'm very much satisfied," Roger said. He crumbled the ashes with the end of a pencil. Mercanton placed a hand on his arm and they went into the dining room.

V

AFTER lunch, Roger drove into Marseille. He was pleased to find Meddling too busy to see him for more than a few minutes. British, French, and American officers swarmed in and out of his office, creating an impressive air of urgency. Roger knew only a few of them. He took a seat in

an obscure corner of the dark entrance hall to wait his
turn, already feeling out of things, isolated in his secret
world. He was interested to observe that the young ser-
geant called Harry had apparently been promoted to serve
as a kind of personal aide to Meddling. He darted about
among the visitors bearing messages from his chief. "Major
Meddling has got those six cartons of cigarettes you asked
for," he said to one British officer. "Major Meddling is
doing what he can about those tires," he told an American
colonel standing near Roger.

Roger knew the form. Payment for services rendered.
There were all kinds of ways of fighting a war. But unless
you were out shooting at the enemy, it all boiled down to
the familiar scramble for what you could get for number
one. He wondered if there wasn't more to it than that, and
if so, why he had lost sight of it. He remembered the sense
of dedication, the devotion to a cause, he had felt when he
first got into it. He must have been an innocent kid, painfully naive. But everything had seemed so clean and
straightforward in the beginning. Now he wasn't so sure.
The shortcomings of his own side were becoming glaringly
obvious. And the other side? Well, there was the Mercanton family. They weren't bad people, really. Of
course, there were always the large issues. But it was hard
to keep your mind on the large issues when you were in
the thick of things. When he was finally ushered into
Meddling's office, Roger found his superior glowing with
confidence and resplendent in an immaculate uniform.

"Jesus Christ, Rog. What've you been up to?" Meddling asked with a show of concern. "You look like hell."

Roger glanced at himself in the mirror behind Meddling's desk. Yes, he did look like hell. His large eyes were darkly circled, and his broad features looked drawn and pinched. His tan was fading, leaving his skin an unhealthy shade of yellow. His ill-fitting civilian suit was shabby and creased.

"I haven't had much sleep," said Roger. "You look as if you were doing all right."

"I've got them eating out of my hand. It's wonderful what you can do with a few cigarettes and a gallon of gas. Nothing goes on around here that I don't know about. Even the British bastards come to me with their troubles. But tell me about our friends in the country. Everything looks pretty good?"

"Yes. It looks fine." Roger handed Meddling the German message. "That came in this morning."

"Great. Great," said Meddling expansively, scarcely glancing at the paper. "I'll wire this right up to Paris and get an answer on it. In the meantime, it's your baby. Paris thinks this might develop into one of the biggest things we have in France. So keep after it."

"Sure. I'll keep after it." As usual, Roger found himself speechless before Meddling's airy self-assurance.

"And another thing, Rog. I want you to have everything you want. Better take some money." Meddling reached into a drawer and pulled out a packet of thousand-franc notes. He tossed it across the desk. "God bless the taxpayer. We've got some more civilian clothes for you, too. Harry'll fix you up. Great boy, Harry. And you better take some food out with you. Anything you want. You might as well be comfortable. Ici, c'est la maison de bon Dieu. That's French, in case you didn't know." Meddling threw his head back and laughed loudly.

With Harry's help, Roger gathered together several boxes of food, including candy and chewing gum for the children. He also took some clothes for himself, mostly rough things suitable for the country. He felt relieved as the big iron gates clanged behind him. He directed his car through the ruins of Marseille towards Aix. Meddling meant well, he told himself, but he just didn't understand. He was fine to work for, in a way. Plenty of money, plenty of food, no questions asked. But that's all it meant to him. You did your job. You lived as well as you could. What more could you want? Roger could never have explained to him the sick revulsion he was beginning to feel when he looked into the eyes of Marthe, or Mercanton, and knew that he was leading them to their destruction. Yes, he was glad to get away from his headquarters, but he didn't look forward to his return to the farm. Now that Mercanton was operating once more, they would settle down to months of intimate collaboration. Months of suspicion, months of wariness, months of dishonesty. Roger was on edge after only five days of it.

VI

HE DROVE slowly, frequently drawing up to the side of the road to observe military traffic, noting the types of vehicles and the insignia they carried. Beyond Aix, he drove past the turning to the Mercanton farm and continued on along the road to Avignon out to a place where he'd heard a field for night fighters had just been established. There, he counted the planes on the ground, and in a brief conversation with a French workman learned that the field was under joint Anglo-American command. As he drove back to La Violette he thought with amusement that he might make a very passable spy. As soon as he reached the Mercanton home, he led Jean Louis into the living room.

"I'd like to get to work on some messages for tomorrow," he said.

"Very good, monsieur." Mercanton hesitated an instant. "Your chief is pleased?"

"Yes. Everybody's very well pleased," he said briskly. "I hope we don't have any more difficulties."

"Ah, I hope so too. I think things will go well from now on."

"Well, let's go. I'm going to read you some information. I want you to imagine you've seen these things yourself. You can arrange them in any way that seems right to you, and write the messages yourself." Roger read off the material he had gathered during the day. Mercanton took notes, asking an occasional question.

"And the date I saw these things?" Mercanton asked when Roger was finished. "I was instructed to give dates whenever possible."

"Well, let's see. You've been out of contact for five days. Let's say you saw some of it three days ago and the rest yesterday and today. And that's another thing. If you feel you ought to, you can give some explanation for why you've failed to make contact."

Mercanton worked rapidly, organizing the information into tight, intelligent telegraphic form. Roger found himself admiring once more his expertness and the workman-like clarity of his mind.

When they were finished and the messages had been encoded, Roger wandered out to the courtyard. It was late afternoon, when the landscape seemed to cast back in radiant color the blasting rays of the sun which it had absorbed all day. Marthe was there surrounded by her chickens. She looked up as Roger came out.

"Ah, monsieur," she called warmly. "That food you brought us. It's wonderful. I haven't seen so much meat all at once for five years."

"I'll bring some out regularly from now on."

"That will be fine. And the chewing gum. The children will love it. I tried some once but it was troublesome. I kept forgetting to chew it. Finally I swallowed it by mistake."

"I believe the man who invented it died of acute indigestion. But Americans thrive on it." They stood contentedly watching the chickens peck at the last bits of grain Marthe threw them.

"There, my pretties," Marthe said after a moment. "Mimosa laid two eggs today. I don't know what's got into her. I was just going for a walk, monsieur. Wouldn't you like to come with me? I like to walk about the place every evening at this time." She picked up a heavy stick leaning against the wall and led the way to a path winding up through the terraced vineyards. After they had climbed for several minutes, Marthe asked idly:

"Do you like the country?"

"Yes, very much. But I've always lived in the city," Roger said. "Do you like it? The country, I mean."

Roger looked at her as he spoke. Despite her simple dress, her flat-soled shoes, and the rough stick which she carried, there was nothing rural about her. The elegant line of her body and the bright cleverness of her face could not be obscured.

"Yes, I love it," she said. "All my life I've always dreamed of having a place in the country. Very much like this. I love this place already. It's very beautiful, don't you think? It's curious it should have worked out the way it has." She spoke thoughtfully, with a trace of wistfulness. Roger felt a sudden deep pity for her and was immediately annoyed with himself. He could not allow his feelings to be involved in this situation.

"You must have an awful lot of work to do," he said clumsily, trying to change the subject. She caught his embarrassment. She looked at him with an odd little smile.

"Yes, but I'm getting used to it," she said. "I don't think it would be convenient to have a servant just now, do you? Come," she said, stepping out ahead of him, "I want to show you something." They had reached the crest of the ridge. Below them they could see the roof of the house, and beyond, the narrow cultivated plain pushing against the grey sullen hills.

"From here on," said Marthe, pointing with her stick, "down this side of the hill and up there and all across the plain, almost as far as you can see—all that belongs to an old woman who lives down there in a little cabin in the valley. She's lived here all her life, saving, working in the fields with her hands, buying up land. She wanted to accumulate a great property for her son. She's very rich now. During the war her son was killed. You will see her.

She often drives by in an old donkey cart to work in one of her fields. I think she's forgotten why she does it. You see, it's not good to plan too far ahead in life." They stood silently looking out over the land.

"You're right," Roger said, softly, moved by her gallantry in spite of himself. "It's very beautiful here." Far down the valley, a tiny village clinging gracefully to the pinnacle of a hill shone white in the paling light of the sun.

"Over there in that town," said Marthe, "they have a saint. They keep her under glass. They say she's grown quite black now but they still have to cut her fingernails regularly. I've read a lot about her since I've been here. Someday, perhaps we could go see her. If I like her, I'm going to make her my patron saint. She is famous mostly for making it rain during the drought. I think I would ask her to do more difficult things."

Roger chuckled. "You think a saint would like to be looked over so carefully before being chosen?" he asked.

"Of course," Marthe answered, smiling. "Because if I do choose her, I shall be very loyal." They were silent again for awhile, watching the dying sun streak the sky with gaudy color, then Marthe asked: "So you think you will stay with us for some time now?"

"Yes, I hope so." Trying to maintain a detached attitude, he added: "Of course, everything depends on your husband's work."

"Yes, of course. You don't know my husband very well, but I think you'll find you can trust him completely."

"I want to." Roger found himself giving way to

Marthe's direct appeal. "I wish I could understand how he happened to get mixed up in this thing."

"It's hard to explain. He never liked the Germans. It was because his work was taken away from him. His work has always been the most important thing in life to him—much more important than me. That was very hard for me to realize when we were first married. When his work was taken away from him I thought he would lose his mind. It was a very bad time. Then this turned up. Even if I had known about it, I don't think I could have stopped him. He had to do something."

"I suppose a lot of people feel that way. Work above all. But there are other things more important."

"Yes, I think there are. But most people spend all their lives finding that out." Marthe hesitated, then went on slowly: "Tell me, monsieur. When your work is finished, what will happen to my husband then?"

There it was. That was the question he must never let them ask. Even he was finding it more and more difficult to face the truth. Now that there was no longer any question about going on with Mercanton, they must all learn to look at life through half-closed eyes—like visitors in a gallery squinting at an abstract painting to see forms that aren't there.

"You understand, I'm not the person that decides such things," he said smoothly. "But if your husband works well for us, I think you can feel sure that everything will be all right."

"Perhaps it would be better if you help us all disappear when the war is over." Marthe spoke lightly, but the thought lodged itself in the back of Roger's mind. Months later, it was to emerge, full-grown and compelling.

VII

THAT evening they had a festive meal. The whole family was excited by the sight of so much food. Even the eldest boy, Dominique, was able to overcome his constricting shyness to join in the holiday atmosphere.

After dinner, when the children had gone to bed, Mercanton carried a huge old phonograph out onto the terrace, where the still night laid a fragile coloring of nostalgia over the jaunty voices of the great French music hall artists.

"I don't know how you feel about such things," Marthe said, as they listened to the records, "but you know, some people don't approve of listening to many of these entertainers now. During the occupation, some of our greatest stars were suspected of working for the Germans. They're blacklisted now."

"That's nonsense," Roger said hastily, aware that they were treading on dangerous ground. "It doesn't hurt to listen to their records. It's like banning Wagner or any other German composer."

"Of course." Mercanton's voice was bitter in the dark. "It's a part of the hysteria of war."

Roger wondered why Marthe had raised the point so tactlessly. She spoke again, explaining herself:

"I agree with you, of course. But I think it best we understand each other about such things. I don't want to offend you."

"I understand," said Roger, liking her now for being out-spoken. He settled deeper into his chair. He was sleepy. He heard Mercanton get up and change the record. This time it was a woman's voice: "La flotte qui roule a l'horizon me fait penser a un garçon qui ne croyait ni Dieu ni di-able." He recognized the voice of Edith Piaff, harsh with the streets, doomed and tormented. "A man who believed in neither God nor the devil." Roger found his eyes clos-ing heavily. He seemed to float in an uncertain state of consciousness. Then he was seized by a hideous fear. A terrible form was pursuing him down an endless corridor. He could make no headway. The creature was gaining on him. "Neither God nor the devil" a voice roared down the corridor. He stumbled and fell. He was lost. The thing was upon him. "Neither God nor the devil" screamed in his ear. He flung his arm back and woke up, his heart pounding. He looked about him in the dark, try-ing to remember where he was. The record was just com-ing to an end on the wheezing phonograph.

"I'm pretty tired," he said. "I think I'd better go to bed."

VIII

THE weeks that followed were, for Roger, a period of adjustment and realignment. Aside from regular trips into Marseille, he spent all his time at the farm. The work with Mercanton developed rapidly, until they were transmitting information to the Germans of real strategic importance. Frequently, Roger didn't know whether it was true or false. It was all dictated from his headquarters—part of an intricate pattern of deception worked out on the highest level of military command. Although Roger received the information already packaged, it was left to him and Mercanton to decide how best to present it so that it was convincing to the Germans. This was work that required constant care and ingenuity. Whether he liked it or not, Roger had to work in the closest possible partnership with Mercanton. Every word they sent had to be checked against the German's knowledge of Mercanton's background and experience.

The Frenchman was fascinated by the intricate game, giving it the best of his energy and well-trained intelligence. He was invaluable in suggesting fictional sources from which he might reasonably be drawing the sort of information which passed through his hands, and he was stern with Roger when the latter tried to gloss over some minor discrepancy. Indeed, it was Mercanton who gave the dominant tone to the work of the team. And that was the way Roger wanted it. It was Mercanton, after all, with whom the Germans supposed they were corresponding.

Together, as the weeks passed, they established a congenial working relationship. Roger was constantly impressed by Mercanton's devotion and single-minded interest, and had no further reason to distrust him. On the basis of incoming messages, Roger was convinced that the Germans regarded Mercanton as a valuable, bona fide agent. There had been no more incidents to arouse Roger's suspicions against his partner. He still worried about the stranger who had appeared so fleetingly at the door of the shed, but Mercanton swore that he was equally mystified, and Roger believed him.

Profoundly troubled by the Judas quality in his relationship with the family, Roger gave much thought to Mercanton's crime. He ended by persuading himself that it had been no crime at all. Mercanton had been victimized by an evil government. He had been led to believe that he was serving Vichy, to which, as the legitimate government of France, he owed unquestioned allegiance. When he felt Mercanton had regained confidence, Roger questioned him about these things. As he listened to Mercanton talking of the dark years when France had been cut off from the outside world, he could understand how reasonable the Frenchman's choice had seemed to him at the time. The Resistance movement appeared to be a Communist effort to penetrate the country at a time of crisis.

"Of course, I'm against Communism," Mercanton said, as he might have said he was against cancer or the seven-year itch. (Roger was against Communism, too. But since the Communists had become his allies, he tried to make excuses for them.) Mercanton had been a spy, yes. But that was a word that cut two ways. Roger's organization employed spies who were among the greatest heroes of the war. Mercanton could have given himself up when the Allies arrived, but the fact that he hadn't was in itself admirable. He had faced a dangerous situation with a sense of duty rather than trying to extricate himself opportunistically.

Above all, Roger liked the man. He had a sort of innocence that was touching. He was always polite, considerate, and immensely conscientious about his work. As a consequence, it was natural that Roger should abandon more and more his carefully prepared defenses, his determination to remain aloof and watchful. And the more he permitted himself to grow attached to Mercanton and his family, the more terrible seemed to him the inevitable conclusion of the affair. A man less sensitive than Chandler might have done the job and not thought of the consequences. But when Mercanton offered him friendship and trust, Roger felt obliged to meet him on the same terms. It wasn't easy. A hundred times a day, he was afflicted by a sense of guilt, of shameful deceit. He didn't even have the consolation of believing that he was acting for the right. On the contrary, the whole thing seemed wrong to him. All right, so you caught a spy. You didn't ask why he was a spy. You shot him. That was the harsh justice of war. But if you chose to work with a man, you contracted an obligation. Mercanton was clearly performing a service of great importance to the Allies. No matter what he had done in the past, he deserved consideration for his current labor.

For Mercanton, life had no complications. As soon as his radio contact had been re-established, and it became evident that he was to figure in a long-term operation, he put the past out of his mind. He was not given to introspection, so his well-disciplined mind simply closed off that chapter of his life, tossing it aside as if it had never happened. Chandler relieved him of all fear for the future. The young American's warm admiration for his work, and his constant emphasis of its importance, were indications enough that everything would work out all right. It seemed to him reasonable that it should. He had been foolish to get involved with the Germans, but after all, if he hadn't he wouldn't be in a position to contribute to Allied success now. He hoped the work wouldn't go on so long that it would interfere with the resumption of his career. He was sometimes annoyed at Chandler's constant presence. He had always been a proud and independent man, and he felt that the American represented an infringement of his liberty, but it was a small price to pay for what might have been a very nasty business.

Actually, Marthe was more affected than her husband by their altered life. She was too perceptive to accept the situation with Mercanton's complete confidence. She was aware of the slight hesitancy that crept into Roger's voice whenever he spoke of the future. Behind her surface composure was a constant dread. Roger himself, however, she found a source of great comfort. They maintained no barriers against each other. It was the first time Marthe had known equality in a close relationship. Although time and habit had dimmed her awareness of it, Mercanton had always stood between her and self-realization. In Roger, she felt an immense release. She could talk to him about anything and find a sympathetic response. He enjoyed her company and was interested and entertained by her opinions. He wasn't aware at first how strong were the ties that were developing between them.

The place itself contributed to the sort of haunted contentment Roger felt all through this time. He loved the farm and the surrounding country. The vintage was just past and there was much work to be done. He joined the couple every day at their chores: pruning the vines, laying down bottles, gathering the last olives and figs. It was work they all enjoyed and it strengthened their feeling of healthy interdependence. Mercanton was naturally silent, but Roger and Marthe joined in teasing him and drawing him out. He soon began to talk more freely and indulge in rather stern little jokes.

Roger brought food, clothing and money from his generous headquarters in Marseille. As the provider, he came to assume undisputed leadership of the family. No decision was taken without its first being approved by him, and unconsciously he accepted the responsibility that this circumstance brought with it.

The younger children took him into their confidence and included him in their games. He was less successful with Dominique.

One evening, little Pierre insisted that the whole family gather round solemnly while he invested Roger with the Order of La Violette. This was an elaborate product of the boy's busy imagination, for which he had created insignia, various ranks, and special decorations. With a rather deficient knowledge of heraldry, he had devised a coat of arms consisting of a flower of uncertain species, a bar sinister, and a rabbit rampant. All the family had been made Chevaliers of the Order, except for Mercanton, who was Grand Maître. The animals had been made Gardiens d'Honneur. For Roger, a special rank had been created, Maître d'État, in recognition of the unique position he held in the family.

"I think your parents might not like that," Marthe commented at the close of the ceremony, regarding the bar sinister pinned to Roger's chest.

Roger made frequent efforts to approach Dominique, but the boy remained tense and sullen, obeying his father's curt commands with barely concealed resentment. Roger was afraid that he had at least a partial notion of what was going on in the house, but there was nothing to be done about it. Although he felt an increasing sense of responsibility for the whole family, he hesitated to interfere directly between father and son.

He and Marthe discovered a mutual interest in the movies, and they frequently drove into Aix in the evening to see a film. At first, Roger felt vaguely perturbed at the violent demonstrations of loathing for the Germans, which took place when the newsreels were shown, but both Marthe and Mercanton joined in so naturally that he quickly got over this feeling. When shots of ruined cities and mass executions were flashed on the screen, Marthe would murmur, "What monsters!" and Mercanton would echo: "It's really shocking." When his astonishment had passed, Roger was pleased with this reaction. It seemed an added proof of Mercanton's good feeling. Roger felt he could possibly help him to a greater awareness of right and wrong, on which to base a new life. Was it too late? Was it ever too late for a man to acknowledge his faults and make amends?

IX

IN OCTOBER, Dominique and Pierre started to school, making the long trip into Aix by bicycle every day. Glad of an added opportunity to make friends with the boy, Roger made it a habit to help Dominique with his English. It was an impulse that he soon regretted.

One morning, after the boys had gone to school, a jeep drove into the courtyard bearing two American MP's and a French gendarme. Roger went out to meet them, his breath forcing its way through a constriction in his chest.

Had the French authorities finally got wind of Mercanton's past? Mercanton was at his side. The gendarme crawled out of the jeep and addressed himself to the older man.

"These soldiers," he said, "they've heard there's an American here. Can you give them any information?"

"An American here?" Roger spoke quickly in his perfect French. He was relieved. It wasn't so bad after all. "What do you mean?"

"You understand, monsieur, it's the American authorities," the gendarme explained. "They're looking for deserters. They've heard there is an American here."

"Just a moment. I'll speak to them," Roger said.

"Ah, you can speak English? That will make it simpler." The gendarme led Roger back to the jeep.

"Good morning," said Roger to the two MP's, speaking English with a faint accent. "What is it you want here?"

"Well, hiya, Mac," said one of the men, "where'd you learn to parlay English?"

"In New York," said Roger. "I lived there many years."

"Well, I'll be damned. I'm from Ohio myself. Ever been there?"

"No, I'm afraid not. Is there anything we can do for you?"

"Sure. The CO heard there was an American out here. Know anything about it?"

"No. Where did your CO hear this story?"

"Oh, some teacher told him one of the kids said he was learning English from an American. So we came out to look around. Got your papers with you?"

"Certainly." Roger produced his identity card and the

permit for his car. The MP took them and handed them over to the gendarme.

"These look OK to you, Frenchie?" he asked. The gendarme studied them and handed them back to Roger. "Everything seems to be in order, monsieur," he said.

"I guess you don't mind if we have a look around. Come on, Bill." The two soldiers descended from the jeep and walked toward the house. Roger followed, thinking of the radio in the closet upstairs, and hoping that Marthe had hidden the Army rations.

"I think I know why there has been this misunderstanding," he said. "I have been teaching one of the boys English myself."

"That so? I guess that's it." The two Americans entered the house, and the others followed, watching as they strolled from room to room.

"Sorry to bother you folks," said the spokesman for the MP's when they'd completed a tour of the ground floor. "We'll just take a look around upstairs and then we'll clear out." Roger and Mercanton followed the two soldiers upstairs. Marthe remained below to pour the gendarme a glass of wine. Roger was thinking fast. If the Americans made too thorough a search, he would be forced to show his credentials, special authorization from Supreme Headquarters. He could imagine the two soldiers talking about it later over drinks, until the story had spread all through the community. He glanced at Mercanton and was answered with anxiously lifted eyebrows.

The MP's passed from room to room, glancing casually in the closets. When they got to his room, Roger walked quickly to the closet, slipped the key into the lock and opened the door. The radio reposed innocently in its suit-case on the floor.

"Not much room here for extra guests," said the articulate MP. "Come on, Bill, let's get going." They returned to the ground floor, where Marthe was conversing brightly with the gendarme. "OK, fellow, we're on our way," said the soldier. He turned to Roger. "Too bad you never got to Ohio. Great country, If you're ever out that way, look me up." The three visitors climbed back into the jeep and drove away.

Roger and Mercanton relaxed with deep sighs of relief, laughing excitedly. Marthe seemed undisturbed.

"That was a very nice gendarme," she said. "Poor man. His little boy was killed when the Americans came. He ran out into the street when some fighting was going on and was hit by a stray bullet."

"From now on," Roger said, "you're in charge of all crises. If any more police come to see us, Jean Louis and I will hide. You can give them wine and listen to their troubles."

"I find it all very interesting," Marthe said with ironic superiority. "He asked me lots of questions about you and my husband. I had no idea how easy it is to lie. I'm afraid I'm learning very bad habits."

When Dominique returned from school that evening, he was severely interrogated by his parents and Roger. He denied ever having described Roger as an American. He had had a dispute in class over the use of an English word and he had quoted Roger as one who had lived in America. He was warned to speak of Roger only with the utmost discretion and he agreed, but there was an odd tight little smile on his lips when he was finally sent about his chores. Roger was worried by the boy. He wondered what might be going on in his mind.

The episode led them all to increase their precautions. Roger had always maintained a watch on the shed and he made regular tours of the whole property, but no one was ever seen on the place except the postman. Marthe had been right—they knew nobody in the community except the tradespeople and the few neighbors with whom they occasionally arranged trades of eggs and other farm produce. But Roger feared the small unexpected mishaps. He drove his car with almost neurotic care, realizing that an accident near the Mercanton home might reveal his identity. He never got over the fear that Mercanton's relations with Vichy might one day lead to trouble with the local authorities. Such little daily worries wore on him, leaving his nerves exposed and over-sensitive. Inevitably, he drew closer to the Mercantons, depending more and more on them for companionship and relaxation.

X

ONE day, shortly after the visit of the MP's, on one of his frequent trips into Aix, Roger was held up on the outskirts of town by a gang of German prisoners working on the road. As he drove slowly around them, his eye was caught by one of the group—a young, sharp-featured German with heavy spectacles. He knew the face instantly. He stopped his car and walked back to the guard, who was seated under a tree alongside the road, a rifle between his legs.

"Tell me," he said. "Do you know anything about that

character over there?" He pointed towards the workers.

"Which one?" the guard asked. "You mean Greuber? Yes, indeed. He gave himself up a couple of weeks ago. He said he was afraid his family would think he was dead if he was reported missing. He'd been living for weeks out in the country."

"Yes, I thought so. I'm sure I saw him wandering around our house not long ago."

"You probably did. I'm sure the country is full of Boches still. I hope they all starve to death. If they don't in the country, they will if they come in to us."

Roger thanked the man and drove on. He could relax his watch on the shed now. If the young German had any connection with the Mercanton case, he was well out of it now. That was one loose end tidied up. He had been right not to mention it to Meddling.

CHAPTER

Six

I

I SAW Roger Chandler again towards the end of October.
I had been sent to Cannes to organize the distribution of
food and medicine in the Cannes-Nice area. For me, it was
a homecoming. I had had a house just outside of Cannes,
towards Theoule, built into the red rocks of the Esterels,
just over the sea. I found it in reasonably good condition.
The Germans had tangled it in barbed wire and had heavily
mined the ground roundabout, but the local commanding
officer very amiably sent over a team of sweepers, and I
was soon able to move in.

The southern front had been stabilized by that time at
Menton, just beyond Monte Carlo. There, the opposing
armies settled in as comfortably as they could and at regular intervals fired guns at each other to remind themselves
that they were, in fact, at war. Sometimes at night, you
could hear the rumble of the artillery at Cannes.

But it was impossible to think seriously of that stretch
of the Riviera as a battle field. It had been too long a play-
ground. The echo of a thousand foolish revelries hung in
the air. The habit of playing host was too deeply ingrained
in the local population. It received the American Army

with a practiced flourish, making the best of the fact that
the new arrivals descended from jeeps and trucks instead
of limousines.

As if by mutual consent, the destruction that had laid
waste the whole coast, from Marseille to St. Raphael,
stopped abruptly on the outskirts of Cannes, and from
there right up to Menton everything remained untouched
and familiar, except for a few unsightly scars in the
neighborhood of Nice. But then, Nice had long since lost
its standing as a smart vacation spot. All the rest—Juan-les-
Pins, Antibes, Villefranche, Cap Ferrat and Monte Carlo
—retained their old allure, a curiously pleasant melange of
hideous hotels, wildly luxuriating foliage, and advertise-
ments for Dubonnet.

I had won the permission of the Army authorities to
use my house as a kind of unofficial officers' club, an in-
formal annex of the elaborate recreation centers being set
up in the great hotels on the Croisette. Through old friends
among the local shopkeepers I was able to keep well
stocked with liquor and managed to pick up enough food
to appease somewhat the apparently insatiable hunger of
my young guests. The place was always crowded, which
made my return easier, for the house was filled with many
memories of my wife.

Major Meddling had been there a number of times. I
understood from him that business brought him frequently
to Cannes. Because the front was stationary, and it was
impossible to patrol the mountainous region back from the
sea, the whole Côte d'Azur was alive with espionage activities. Agents passed quite freely from one side to the other.
The local population offered limitless opportunities for cor-

ruption. Its background of pimping and procuring was so extensive that it would have been astonishing had there been any scruples about selling military intelligence to either side.

When I found Roger walking down the rue d'Antibes one day, I supposed that some such business had brought him to Cannes. I was delighted to see him. He had made a strong impression on me during our trip from Naples, and I had hoped we might run across each other again. He explained that he had come to Cannes for a couple of days' vacation. He had an appointment to meet Meddling later in the day for a business talk, but otherwise his time was free. I asked him to come out to my house that evening and he promised he would. As we talked I felt a tension in him I hadn't noticed before. He seemed restrained and preoccupied. I missed the buoyant laughter that had so cheered our invasion voyage. But he had still that quality of purposeful directness that I had found so striking on shipboard. We parted after a few moments' chat.

II

ROGER met Meddling that afternoon at the Carlton, where his chief was occupying a suite. I heard about their conversation later. Meddling was in his usual heavy-handed good spirits.

"Great to see you, Rog," he said in greeting. "I want to hear all about things in the country."

"Nothing much to tell. I suppose you've been seeing my reports every week," Roger said. He went on to fill in details and bring Meddling up to date on the progress of the work. When he was finished, Meddling said: "It's settled down into pretty much of a routine, huh?"

"Yes, I think I've got it pretty well set up."

"That's it, Rog. You've done a great job. Tell you what I was thinking. We've got new cases coming up all the time. You're the best man I've got to handle them. How about letting one of the other boys take over in the country so you can come in and help me out?"

Roger was stunned. Such a possibility had never occurred to him. He was startled at the vigor with which he rejected the idea. He remembered how reluctant he had been to carry on with the case just a few weeks ago. But things had changed. He knew the family now, and was fond of all of them. He couldn't imagine anyone else taking his place in the household. They needed him. He was committed to them.

"I don't see how you can do that," he said, trying to keep his voice casual. "If you put somebody else out there, the whole tone of the messages might change."

"Well, as I understand it, this fellow Mercanton is a pretty smart guy. Now that you've got everything working so well, somebody else could just follow the routine you've established. I need you with me, Rog."

"It's not as simple as that." Roger's voice was growing sharp. "It's all very well to talk about routine. But there're a thousand details you've got to watch constantly. I understand Mercanton. We've learned how to work together. Anybody else would blow the whole works."

"Hell, I know you've done a damn fine job," Meddling said placatingly. He hated disagreements with his subordinates. He liked to think of his unit as a happy family laboring under his benevolent supervision. "It's just that it seems to me that you're wasting your time now that the difficult part of the job is finished."

"I don't agree with you. I don't think the difficulties will be over until . . ." Roger paused instinctively.

"Until our friend is introduced to the executioner?" Meddling laughed. "Well, you know me, Rog. I want to work things out the way you think best. If you want to, stay out there for awhile longer. But I can't promise to leave you indefinitely. Something may turn up. I may need you for another job."

Roger was satisfied for the moment. But the conversation set his mind working in new directions. For the first time he realized that in some way he had become bound to the Mercantons. He had accepted responsibility for them. They were his problem now. He must stay with them until their tragedy was played out. This brief holiday was possible because Mercanton was not transmitting, allowing time for a fictional visit to Marseille to gather information. It was the first time he had dared leave the farm for so long. But now he felt a sudden impatience to return. He knew why. This was more than a job. His feelings were hopelessly involved.

When Chandler arrived at my house that evening, Meddling was with him. They were early and there were only a few other men there. I made the introductions and passed drinks around, and we all settled down on the terrace over the sea to watch the sunset.

Meddling treated Roger with the patronizing camaraderie that was characteristic of him. "Roger's been working too hard," he said to me. "I hope you'll keep an eye on him while he's here. Show him a good time."

"I think Roger knows this place as well as I do," I said. "There's probably not much I can show him."

"Hell, that's right. I forgot he was one of the original members of the international set. How about it, Rog? You really going to cut loose while you're here?"

"I'll do my best, George," Roger said casually. "I haven't got much time."

"Now, look here. I want you to forget all about that business for awhile. That's an order. You can afford to take a few days off."

"OK, George. We'll see how things go," said Roger without enthusiasm.

"There. You see what I mean?" Meddling addressed the whole group. "The best man I've got. And what happens? The minute I let him out of my sight he goes off and falls in love with a bunch of bums. I can't do anything with him."

"Let's let it go." Roger rose abruptly and strolled off to the other end of the terrace. I had frequently noticed Meddling's blissful lack of sensitivity to other people's feelings, but I was puzzled by Roger's behavior. It seemed to me that Meddling, in his tiresome way, was trying to be kind. But Roger's departure was an act of deliberate rudeness. I saw a look of surprised resentment pass over Meddling's face, but he was not the sort to take offense easily and we were all soon talking of other things.

Roger remained subdued during the rest of the evening. When people were beginning to leave, I looked around for him and finally found him alone out on the terrace gazing down at the sea. It was a lovely clear night of bright moonlight, but bitterly cold. Down towards Monte Carlo the sky was lighted by occasional flashes, and we could hear from time to time the boom of the guns.

"Are you watching our war?" I asked.

"Yeah. Does that go on often?" He spoke as if to himself, scarcely aware of my presence.

"Every night, I believe. You can't always see it."

"Very pretty fireworks. I suppose people are being killed down there."

"Yes, I suppose so. But not very many. Can you think of many places where people aren't being killed?"

"Mmm. Cheerful thought."

"Cheerful world. Aren't you freezing? Come on in and have a drink by the fire."

When we got back to the living room, we found that everybody had left. We settled ourselves in deep armchairs on either side of the fireplace. Roger's large eyes were thoughtful and he sat silently for some time looking into the fire.

"This is a hell of a war," he said at last, smiling faintly.

"The last one wasn't very entertaining, either," I said. He looked up at me, the smile fading.

"I'm sorry," he said. "I suppose I'm being pretty childish. I'm upset."

"What's the matter? Having trouble with Meddling?"

"Oh, that. I'm sorry about that, too. No, he just annoys the hell out of me sometimes without meaning to. I shouldn't let him bother me. Well, I'd better clear out and let you get some sleep." He made no move to rise.

"There's no hurry. Old men don't need much sleep, you know. Something's on your mind. Can I help you?"

"No. I wish you could." He was gazing into the fire once more.

"Why don't you tell me about it?"

"It's a long story. Besides, it's a military secret." He addressed the fire mockingly.

"Well, in that case . . ."

"Oh, the hell with it." He looked at me a long moment. "Goddam it, I've got to talk it over with someone. You brought this on yourself."

III

So ROGER told me much of what I've already set down. He didn't mention names or places, and he was vague about the nature of his work, but I was able to fill in many gaps with the knowledge I already had of the intelligence service. I suppose it was a serious indiscretion for him to have spoken of the affair at all, but he was anxious to share his burden and I hoped that I might be able to help him. When he had finished his account, I asked: "Just what is it that's bothering you in all this?"

"Jesus Christ, don't you understand?" he demanded, with torment in his voice. "What's it all about. We're fighting Nazism, but these people aren't Nazis. They're damn nice. They're a lot better than average."

"Good God, you didn't expect the enemy to be composed entirely of monsters, did you? There're lots of nice people on the other side. Some very good friends of mine were on the wrong side in France."

"That's just it. If this sort of thing had happened in the States, I can imagine my father and a lot of my friends winding up in the same fix."

"I can too. But that doesn't make them right."

"Of course not. But it makes the whole thing such damn dirty hypocrisy. We have no right to judge these people."

"Ha. That sounds pretty naïve. Don't misunderstand me. I think you've got a very tough job on your hands. The most gruesome story I ever heard about the last war was the one about the Christmas Eve when German and Allied troops climbed out of their trenches and met out in No Man's Land to drink together and exchange season's greetings. When the party was over they went back to their trenches and a little later they were all blazing away at each other. I don't like that story. I hope it isn't true. There're not many men you'd want to kill after you'd had a drink together. War's got to be kept impersonal, or we'd all have to face the fact that we're cold-blooded murderers. And that's not a realization that's good for the soul."

"So what's the answer? We should all pack up and go home?"

"No, no, no. It's right that we went to war when we did. If nothing else, it was a question of practical necessity. But when we say that we're fighting to destroy oppression, we're telling ourselves lies. And by lying to ourselves, we falsify everything we do. If we admitted that we're fighting to save our own skins, it'd be better. Hitler didn't happen in 1939. He was around a long time, and we looked the other way as long as it was convenient. As far as that goes, there's plenty of oppression being practiced right now by us and our allies, both at home and abroad. And we don't choose to do anything about it. It's our confusion of motives that embarrasses us when we go to war. We like to feel we have awfully good reasons for killing people. So we adopt a set of lofty ideals as our own and endow the enemy with every black-hearted trait we can think of. But when we come face to face with the enemy and find him acting according to a set of standards that isn't very different from our own, it's apt to be upsetting."

"That's just it. Our own record isn't good enough. We haven't the right to judge others by a standard we don't adhere to ourselves."

"That's true obviously. That leaves us only one course. We should acknowledge all our past wrongs and begin behaving in a way that fits our fine talk. It's the only way to justify our position as conqueror and judge."

"Do you really see any signs of that happening?" Roger demanded impatiently.

"No," I replied honestly.

"Well, then, what are we talking about?"

"Try to look at it this way. Statesmanship, world affairs, everything leads back to the individual. Start there. Man's relationship to man. Man's failure to fulfill the goodness in him is magnified and distorted in the state. We'll have conflict on a world scale as long as you and I try to take advantage of our fellows. When we care enough about our neighbor to defend actively his right to a complete life, regardless of whether he's black, white or half-tone—that is to say, without prejudice—then the world will grow more agreeable. Not before. We're paying now for our carelessness of the individual. The individual failure to recognize an obligation to all men—that's the enemy we should seek out, in peace and in war."

"All right. Where do we go from there? You're convincing me that a man like Meddling is more to be feared than my friend in the country."

"He probably is. But you can't start fighting him. That's one of the worst things about war. You have to learn to make friends with evil. But I'm not finished."

I tried to point out to him that Mercanton's crime was one against humanity. It had very little to do with his radio espionage. It seemed to me that any man so unaware of his fellow's well-being as to accept racism, the enslavement of workers, and all the rest of the rightist, totalitarian doctrine, deserved anything that happened to him. Ignorance was no excuse. The world hadn't burst into conflict overnight. It had been every man's duty to choose sides in the tortured years that preceded the final catastrophe. His duty to himself, and his duty to his neighbors. But even as I spoke, I realized that I was condemning the vast majority of mankind. So few had made the imperative choice. And was it fair to expect people to choose, with the world so gripped by ignorance, prejudice, and powerful interests who strove to keep it so? I could see Roger's point. Mercanton's crime was unimportant compared to the similar crimes of men in high places who had executed neat volte-faces as the war progressed, and still enjoyed the respect of the world. It was curious justice that permitted punishment of one and let the others go scot free.

But Chandler seemed to be striving to achieve the impossible. He apparently felt impelled to assume responsibility for Mercanton's wrong. I tried to explain to him that people must accept the consequences of their own acts. But always I was confronted by his devoted faith in these people. His affection for them distorted his perspective. Because they shared with him similar tastes and background, offered him kindness and a picture of happy domesticity, he surrendered his judgment. He couldn't imagine an evil ideology growing in an atmosphere of such simple virtue.

Oh, we talked a great deal and I knew it was a waste of time. Roger kept leading the conversation back to his friends in the country. The warmth with which he spoke of them disturbed me. It seemed to me inevitable that Chandler would be deeply hurt before he was free of this family. If, indeed, he was ever free of it.

IV

DURING his short holiday in Cannes, Chandler met a girl called Danielle Segher. I knew her well, and it was she who told me later something of this meeting.

Roger was sitting alone on the terrace of the Carlton bar, the morning after our talk, when he became aware that the conversation around him had changed in pitch. It was the sort of shift in key that takes place in any polite gathering when something startling occurs which should not be openly acknowledged. It is the well-bred substitute for the pointed finger. He looked up and saw that the attention of his neighbors was fixed covertly on a dark girl standing near the steps at the end of the terrace. She was looking about her, as if searching for someone. He noticed only that she was simply, almost severely dressed, in a plain white blouse, soft grey tweed skirt and flat-soled sandals.

As she started to move down between the tables, he saw several people rise and greet her. She moved with authority, pausing briefly, exchanging a few words, occasionally smiling a quick frank smile that exposed startlingly white, even teeth. Roger watched her approach. He could see now that she wore very little make-up. Her hair was dark brown and combed back casually to her shoulders. Her skin was dark, the coloring heightened by the sun. Her height was average, not noticeably short or tall. She was slim, but well-proportioned. As she neared Roger's table, he noticed a sleek, shrewd little Frenchman half rise to speak to her, but she quickened her pace and brushed past him, as if not seeing him. She sat down alone at a table next to Roger's.

As soon as she was seated, he was aware that conversation on the terrace had resumed its normal level. He looked over at her, wondering why she should cause such a stir. Her features were small—level eyebrows and wide-set, rather almond-shaped eyes that gave her face an intense, almost winged look; a short, brisk nose; a wide, full mouth that was too big for the rest of her face and gave it a merry lack of balance. Roger guessed her age at about twenty, though her movements were mature and decisive. Despite this, and the lack of jewelry and make-up, there was something dainty about her, delicately feminine. He was still studying her when she glanced up and caught his eye. He was briefly embarrassed at being caught so obviously staring, but he smiled and leaned forward.

"Won't you have a drink?" he asked. She looked at him disinterestedly for a moment, not rudely but with curiosity, studying him. Then her face broke into her sudden whole-hearted smile and she looked him directly in the eye.

"Yes, I'd like it very much," she said. Roger felt an agreeable tingle pass through him. She was unlike anyone he'd ever known. She stood up, stepped over to his table and sat down opposite him. It was an easy rapid move-ment, so that Roger didn't have time to rise and fumble with her chair. She met his eye once more. Roger smiled back at her.

"What will you have?" he asked.

"Whatever you're having."

"You're easy to please." Roger signalled the waiter and turned back to the girl. "Do you always cause so much excitement when you appear in public?"

"How do you mean? Oh, when I arrived? No, I'm not used to it myself." They had been speaking French, but the girl suddenly switched to English.

"Good Lord, you *are* French, aren't you?" Roger asked. "Should I know you? Are you a movie star or something?"

"What a lot of questions." The girl chuckled delight-edly. "Yes, I'm French. My name is Danielle Segher. And I'm not a movie star. I worked in the underground during the occupation. These people have just found out. I think some of them are a little frightened of me. That's all."

"And that man over there," Rogers pointed at the sleek little Frenchman whom Danielle had cut. "Is he one of the ones who's frightened of you?"

"Oh, that horrid little creature. He's tried to work for every side." For an instant her expression became almost forbidding. Then she glanced up at Roger and smiled. "Did you notice me cut him?" she asked with naïve delight.

"I noticed everything you did," Roger said.

They chatted some more, exchanging brief autobiographies. She was the daughter of a wealthy French family that had moved to Cannes from the Occupied Zone after the Armistice in 1940. She told Roger little about her war work, but the story was familiar to those of us who had known her at the time. Without saying anything to her family, whose sympathies were uncertain, she had made contact with the Resistance. At first, she was given unimportant jobs, but she soon won the confidence of her chiefs and by the time the Germans moved into the south of France she was doing some of the most important underground work in the area. She used to bicycle innocently up and down the coast, radio parts concealed in the basket strapped to her handlebars, supplying her colleagues. She was in regular contact with England, and was responsible for the escape of many British flyers. The position of her family gave her special protection, but I confess I was surprised to find her still alive when I returned to Cannes. Her work was now finished. She had grown very restless, trying, for lack of anything else to do, to fit herself back into the elaborate, conventional social life of her family.

After they had talked for some time, Roger looked at his watch.

"Look, why don't you have lunch with me?" he suggested. "It's Army food but I have a good cook."

"I suppose this is where nice girls are supposed to say, 'Well, I really have an engagement.' But I'd love it. I haven't a thing to do 'til after lunch. Do you have a house here?"

"Come on. I'll show you."

Roger was staying in a big old villa in Californie, on the hill in back of Cannes. It belonged to friends of his family. He had found the caretakers still in residence, and they had insisted he would be more comfortable here than in one of the requisitioned hotels in town.

As they drove up the steep winding drive, Danielle exclaimed: "But this is the Johnson's villa. I used to come to children's parties here when I was little."

"That so? So did I, once or twice. They were awful parties, as I remember."

"They must have been awful for the boys. I remember they were very dressed up and formal, very proper imitations of the parties our parents went to. Well, there won't be any more parties like them. You can thank the war for that."

"No more parties? Why not?"

"Who's going to give them? That whole class of people are being destroyed by the war. In the new social order, there won't be any room for that sort of training in snobbery." In the course of her war work she had acquired the habit of larding her conversation with patches of social or political doctrine. It was an appealing trick. She became very earnest and seemed to be trying, without much success, to shed her femininity.

"You really believe that?" Roger demanded with a trace of bitterness. He was fed up with the pious notion that the war was accomplishing some good. And his one-sided relationship with the Mercantons was beginning to make him impatient with all disagreement. On the farm, his word was law. He was learning to expect deference to his opinion. "You know, being here again makes me wonder if there ever was a war. People aren't even waiting for the guns to stop firing before they pick up right where they left off. But don't let's talk about the war. I'd like to forget it."

"You too?" She laughed at him teasingly.

They had lunch on the terrace, looking down on the trim harbor, which the Germans had made less lovely by playfully sinking all the yachts at anchor there. Their masts stuck out of the water like an intricate maze of channel markers. The sweep of the sea was broken to the west by the sharp form of the Esterels. Although the rainy season had started, the sky was clear and fresh.

As they talked, Roger let his eyes wander over the girl opposite him, feeling within him the mysterious appeal of her small round breasts as they pressed against the edge of the table, observing with deep pleasure the curve of her mouth, soft and tender, the graceful line of her neck as it flowed into her shoulders. Sometimes their eyes met and held across the table, and they fell silent. Roger's hands were restless with the desire to know the feel of her, to encompass her in his touch. She too was curiously stirred by the American. She felt no impulse to erect guards against him.

As soon as lunch was over Roger rose abruptly and moved vaguely over to the railing of the terrace. He would have to take care. He didn't want to go too far. He had so little time. She sat still, waiting for him to turn back to her, wondering why he had withdrawn from her. She looked across at him as he stood with his back turned, drawn by the solidity of his shoulders, the power of his legs and buttocks.

"What are you planning to do this afternoon," he said at last, indifferently, his back still turned to her.

"I have a number of things to do in town. And I promised to meet some people later on." She responded coldly to his manner, at the same time hesitating to break from him completely. He turned to her, suddenly reluctant to let her go.

"You could put that off to some other time. Why don't we do something together? I'm not going to be here long, you know."

"Well, I don't know. There are things I really ought to do." Her pride was aroused now, warning her not to give herself away.

"If there're chores you have to do, I could drive you. We could do something together afterwards."

"Yes, that might be all right. What do you want to do?" She spoke without enthusiasm, allowing herself to be persuaded.

"I don't know. What is there to do? We could drive up to the front and take a shot at the Boches." He felt free for the moment, basking in the warmth of her attraction.

"All right. Do you have a gun? I'm a good shot." She sprang up, smiling, and tucked in her blouse. She stood facing him, her head thrown back, her feet a little apart, her weight thrown back on her heels. Her eyes were laughing, challenging him. This had some of the excitement of old times. Life had seemed unaccountably dull since her part in the war had ended. She missed the thrilling immediacy of her work. Her reaction to this young

American lifted her out of herself, charged her once more with a piercing vitality.

Roger moved quickly to her side and took her hand, smiling down at her. They went out hand in hand and got into the Renault.

"Very well, mademoiselle, where do you have to stop first?" Roger demanded.

"Oh, don't let's bother with anything. I'll be irresponsible. Let's just drive." She spoke gaily. The tension between them had evaporated. Sitting beside him, she felt now a great restful contentment.

They drove down the coast, through Nice and on to Monte Carlo, chatting aimlessly and admiring the generous splendor of the landscape. Roger had to present his special papers to pass the numerous road patrols.

"This is the first time I've been to Monte Carlo since before the war," said Danielle. "You must be very important to get past all these military police. Maybe *you're* a movie star."

"No. But I've got papers signed by an important person. That makes a difference."

"Now do we go shoot Germans?"

"No. I don't think even these papers would help much up there. I've got a better idea." They drove through the expensive glitter of Monte Carlo and cut back into the hills, climbing steeply to La Turbie, where a Roman emperor once erected a colossal shaft to commemorate a victory over the Gauls. They left the car and walked past the monument to the crest of the ridge. Far below them lay Monte Carlo, a pretty toy town embraced by the sea. From this height, they could look across the intervening ridges down into Italy. They sat side by side on the sun-warmed ground, Olympians gazing down at man's folly.

"Well, there's your war," said Roger. "From here, we could almost drop stones on the Germans. It doesn't look very terrifying, does it?"

"Oh, but it is. It's so beautiful here. And so peaceful. We're so close to it, and yet we seem so safe. I think that's terrifying."

He handed her a cigarette and offered her a light from his lighter. Their eyes met across the flame. He snapped the lighter shut, keeping his eyes on hers. She took the cigarette from her lips. He leaned towards her and kissed her on the mouth, tasting the faint sharpness of the tobacco. She opened her mouth to his. He drew her into him. His hands slipped over the silk stuff of her blouse, learning the substance of her. She felt slight and young in his arms. She seemed to be holding back nothing of herself. She lay against him breathless, caught up in him, unaware of time or place, transported and yielding.

Roger opened his eyes and looked at the girl's face pressed against his. Her eyes were closed and he watched the blind fluttering of her lids. It made him feel remote from her—shut off from the private activity of the mind behind the veiled eyes. The lids parted slowly and Danielle half opened her eyes. Roger's heart seemed to stop beating. They looked, unresisting, in upon each other. Some deep layer of feeling was touched in him and he was aware of teetering out of space, as if he were losing his balance and falling . . . falling into the very depths of her. The need for her, the acceptance of her, swept through him with the impact of a physical sensation, and he could feel it spreading down through his arms into his hands, passing warmly through his whole body. He closed his eyes, reeling with what he had seen.

"You're wonderful," he said, keeping his mouth on hers. She made a slight movement towards him, as if gathering all of herself into his arms. It seemed to him an almost stifling movement, and the tumult subsided within him. He felt as if a door had been closed behind him, a retreat cut off. A vague conflict stirred in him and he drew gently away from the girl.

Danielle felt the urgency drain away from them and she sat up, keeping her head turned slightly away from him, rudely flung back upon herself. He sat still, making no further move towards her. She plucked idly at a blade of grass, deserted and bewildered. What had she done? Where was this leading? She couldn't understand Roger's sudden advances and withdrawals. In a woman, they could have been dismissed as traditional feminine guile. Something was wrong between them. What was it? She stole a glance at Roger. He was staring down into the hills before him, his face expressionless. He was apparently going to let matters rest as they were. A gust of wind brushed the hair back from her cheek. She felt forlorn now, sitting on this majestic eminence.

"Let's go back," she said dully. "It will be cold soon."

They went back to the car and drove down the way they had come. Neither spoke. He knew he had destroyed something, allowed a moment to pass. He wanted to say something to her, offer some explanation. But no words came. He wanted her terribly but he couldn't complicate his life further. He knew she wouldn't take it lightly.

That was the trouble. He told himself that there was something demanding about her, as if she might encompass his life. It was impossible for him to realize that his experience with the Mercantons was leading him to avoid the give and take, the mutual surrender, of a complete relationship. As they approached Cannes, he finally spoke:

"Will you have dinner with me?" he asked. Regret had begun to take the place of his momentary urge to be free of her. He hoped she would say yes. It was growing dark and the night's chill was in the air. He felt loneliness weighting his spirit. He thought of the overwhelming tenderness of their moment on the hillside. He was angry with himself for having rejected it.

"Haven't you things you ought to do?" she asked, remote and still.

"Nothing at all. I wish you'd come."

"Oh, very well. I'll have to make some phone calls." As soon as she had spoken she regretted it. What was the use? Something stood between them. It would be more sensible to go home and try to forget it. She huddled miserably in the corner of the seat.

Back at the borrowed villa, they both felt self-conscious and a trifle alarmed in the shadowy intimacy of the great disused drawing room. Its imitation marble columns looked like part of some abandoned stage setting. Most of the furniture remained in dust covers. They avoided each other's eyes, aware of the revelation they had glimpsed in each other a little while before.

Dark had fallen rapidly outside. Roger lighted a fire, making bright conversation all the while, hoping that the warmth would in some mystic way lead them back to the contact which he had so roughly severed. He put a record on the phonograph and the jolly swirling music of an accordion filled the room.

"Come on," he said. "Let's see if you're a real Frenchman." He caught her in his arms and they sped around the room in the tight little circles of the Paris dance halls. When the music ended, they stood close together, laughing, a little out of breath.

"I don't think I'd bother with a man who couldn't do that," Danielle said. She fell into a deep chair close to the fire. "That was fine."

Roger sprawled in a chair beside her. They both felt suddenly released. They were sure of each other again, without constraint. They turned their backs to the room and felt enclosed and protected by the circle of light thrown off by the fire. All at once, they had a great deal to say to one another. Talk spilled from them, direct and easy. Their day together was fulfilled in this moment. Roger kept his eyes on the girl, delighting in her vigor, absorbed by the intensity that was accented by her slightly slanted eyes, her bold mouth.

They talked of the past, of their families, of their plans for the future, exploring each other, offering each other their secrets and their dreams. Danielle felt a sharp pang of pleasure every time she heard Roger's full joyful laughter. It was all right. He had accepted her. She had been foolish to be upset by his earlier brief mood.

When it was time to eat, they had the table set up in front of the fireplace. The old Frenchwoman who served them was bridling with pleasure.

"This is a little like old times," she said. "It's been

a long time since there was any happiness in this house."

"The war's almost over, now," said Roger. "Everything will be like old times soon."

"God grant that it's soon," the old woman said. She brought them a bottle of good wine with their meal, and produced a bottle of champagne with the dessert.

"I hope the Johnsons won't mind," said Roger.

"Oh, the Johnsons won't know anything about it. We were saving this for the end of the war, but I think this is a good time to celebrate."

"It's very good of you, Marie," said Roger.

"It's nothing. Is the young lady staying for breakfast?" The woman laughed roguishly. "I think you ought to invite her for breakfast."

"Get out, Marie," Roger said with mock anger. "You're embarrassing the girl." They all laughed and the woman withdrew. Roger turned to Danielle.

"Will you stay for breakfast?" he asked, smiling. The girl was looking down at her plate. After a moment, she looked up.

"Yes," she said, softly. "If you want me."

The smile faded from Roger's lips as he met her eyes.

V

UPSTAIRS in the bathroom, preparing for bed, Danielle thought of the other times this had happened. It was inevitable that it should have happened before. She had worked with many young men, faced death with them, shared their danger and their paralyzing fear. It was natural that there had been times when she had shared their

moments of relief, too, the brief interludes of replenish-
ment. But this was different. Her feeling for Roger was
complete and startling. She could admit it now. She had
known it when she first met him this morning. He was
peace and a wild excitement and the fulfillment of a quest.
He shared her rebellion against a common background.
Something within her flesh seemed to reach out for him.

She snapped off the light and opened the door. She stood
in the doorway naked, her slim body outlined in the light
of the small lamp by the bed. Roger was sitting on the
side of the bed, wearing a light robe. He stood up quickly
and slipped it off. He crossed to her. She watched the
shadows play across the flat muscles of his chest and
stomach. She caught her breath as his body closed to hers.
She could feel him rigid against her. Their mouths met
and a convulsion threw their bodies tight against each
other. She could feel his hands travelling down her back,
his long fingers close around her waist. He lifted her
slightly from the floor, holding her flat against him, and
carried her to the bed. He laid her down gently. He stood
over her, held by her eyes. He felt again the curious plung-
ing sensation he had known that afternoon, losing his balance, sinking through to the very core of her. He lay down
beside her and she gathered him into her arms with a little
cry. For an instant he was numb with the shock of possession. Even when physical sensations began to return to
him, he was scarcely conscious of them. He was carried
beyond physical awareness, immersed in the essence of the
girl, in her quality of being. He ceased to exist within himself. Everything was forgotten. For both of them, the
whole world lay shimmering within their embrace. They

made love instinctively, graspingly, heedless of their act, striving to attain the impossible fusion, until, shuddering, they broke beyond the boundaries of self.

Roger lay wide awake, shaken by the immensity of their experience. It was beyond anything he had ever imagined. There had been an overwhelming release, but now he was alone again, shut off by a stubborn denial. Their coming together had been clean and simple, with the purity of complete physical acceptance. He tried to put a label on his feelings for Danielle, but something in him drew back. A shadow lay between them. Was it simply because he felt his time was not his own? He thought of the family in the country. He must return to them tomorrow. Good. He felt he owed them the best of himself. But there was no reason why he should allow them to come between him and Danielle. This was the first time in months he had been able to act naturally, without calculation.

Then why should it be so difficult? What was the quality in her that he felt he must fight? He thought briefly of Carol. But the memory of her was cold and without substance. He had never felt like this about Carol. She had nothing to do with this. And he owed her nothing. Their engagement had never been officially announced. Danielle was the sort of girl he had always wanted. If only she wouldn't try to tie him down. He must guard his freedom. He rolled over and lay against her, his mouth against her breast. She laid a hand on his face, holding him to her, lightly sketching the outline of his features with her fingers.

"You know, I'm very much in love with you," she said simply.

"And I love you. Don't talk. Let's go to sleep like this."

VI

THEY were up early the next morning. It was another day of bright sunshine. They had breakfast on the terrace, delighting old Marie with their presence. Roger wore only a pair of shorts. After breakfast they walked into the grounds, which rose steeply in back of the house. After climbing for several minutes up a thickly wooded path, they came out on a small grassy dell enclosed in a high hedge, with a summer house at one end. They sat on the grass, Roger sprawling to receive the sun. They were silent, shy with the intimacy of the night before. It had been bigger than anything either of them had ever known. Both of them were afraid to say anything, afraid to jar the ecstatic memory with the wrong word. Each was a little in awe of the other. They had given each other so much of themselves. They had to grow used to it slowly. They both felt as if they had received a wonderful gift that might be taken away from them. Roger stretched out his hand and let it run caressingly down Danielle's arm. She took it and twined her fingers in his.

"What a wonderful day," she said gaily. "Everything's wonderful. I'm happy."

"So am I."

"I'm glad. But I'm so happy, I don't see how you could help yourself. You're pretty lucky to have such a happy girl."

"Sure I'm lucky." He laughed but he wished she would leave it alone. He didn't want to feel hemmed in by their love. Women were apt to be like that. But some of them weren't. There was. . . . Well, there was Marthe. She was easy and understanding and knew when to retire into the background. Of course, he wasn't in love with Marthe, but it was a quality you could feel. He spoke again, in a rather injured tone:

"You know, I have to go away today."

"Even that doesn't depress me. At least, not much," she added more soberly. "Will you be going far?"

"Pretty far."

"Will you be in danger?"

"No, of course not."

"Will you write to me?"

"I'll try, but I may not be able to." Roger instinctively avoided her questions. His training in secrecy made it impossible to discuss his movements freely.

"Can I write to you?" Danielle began to feel she was conducting an inquisition, but it was right for her to know these things.

"Not possibly."

"Well, that's one definite answer anyway." She tried not to be hurt by his bare responses. "I suppose I will see you again someday."

"Of course. I don't know when, but soon." He heard the troubled note in her voice. Well, she might as well learn how things had to be. He drew her to him and unbuttoned the front of her dress. She wore nothing underneath. Her breasts trembled under his hand. "Take this off," he said softly. She stood up and slipped out of her dress. Roger took off his shorts and went to her. Her body was golden and perfect in the sun.

"Wait. Let me look at you," she said holding him from

her. "What silly little hairs you have on your chest. You're not a man. You're just a little boy."

"You think so?" said Roger and pulled her to him. She slipped out of his arms and ran from him. He ran after her and seized her and they fell to the warm ground laughing, their senses tingling with delight in each other.

They rolled about together, roughhousing and covering each other's bodies with kisses, glorying in the sun and earth, in each other and their own nakedness. When they lay still at last, panting and exultant, he took her to him once more, this time slowly and gently, looking into her eyes, until the tension within both of them overwhelmed them and they reeled in trembling union.

Later in the morning, Roger drove the girl home. They sat close together in the car, rarely speaking. A little while ago they had been gloriously together, but now that it was time to return to work, Roger was impatient to be off.

"It's hard saying good-by," Danielle said as they drove up to her house.

"We don't have to. I'll see you soon," Roger said lightly, trying to cover his haste.

"Well, I'll be dreaming of you and waiting for you."

"It won't be long." He knew it was a lame reply. But he had to get away. If she felt his inattention, she would only misunderstand. He couldn't bear to hurt her. It was just that he had to have time to think things out. He kissed her hurriedly and urged her with a slight pressure towards the door. She looked at him for a long moment and then jumped out of the car and ran into the house.

Roger drove out of Cannes and set his car on the road to Aix.

CHAPTER
Seven

ﭩﭩ

I

Once on his way to the farm, he wished he were back with Danielle. There were still so many things they had to say to each other. So many things to learn about each other. Was it possible that he had met her only yesterday morning? A lot had happened in that brief time. She had become a part of him. Through her, his life had taken on another dimension, a whole new direction. Now that he was away from her he could feel it. He had been an idiot to spoil some of their time together. But that sort of thing was bound to happen at the beginning. It didn't mean anything. God, he would miss her. It was tough having to be separated like this. It wouldn't make his job any easier, either. He couldn't afford to grow careless about the job. Thinking this, he made an effort to concentrate on the road.

Whenever he returned to La Violette, even after a short absence, Roger's mind automatically sprang to attention, his senses alert to signs of danger or disaster. This time, he felt obliged to be doubly watchful, for he had never before been away so long. He drove as fast as he dared the last few miles, anxiety pressing him on.

When he reached the farm, the family was delighted to see him. They received him with an undisguised pleasure that drove Danielle into the back of his mind. Strange how this place had become home for him. Everything about it was familiar and right. He was happy to be back. It was good to be with people who trusted you and made no demands. He felt a great warmth towards them all.

They stood about him in the courtyard asking him questions about his trip, while little Pensée dashed about, barking hysterically. He had become their only contact with the outside world, so there was much they wanted to know about the Riviera and what damage the Germans had done, and whether this or that landmark was still standing. When the first excitement of Roger's arrival had worn off, Marthe said:

"But we have news for you. Pensée has found a lover. I think we did her an injustice. She's turning into a lady dog. She has a friend that comes to see her every afternoon. But that's not all. . . ."

"No. We have something really important to show you," said Mercanton, his eyes shining with secret pleasure. "Come inside."

They left the children and went into the living room. Mercanton went to the desk and took from one of the drawers a package wrapped in brown paper. He drew away the paper, revealing three cloth-bound books. "There you are," he said, enjoying his little drama.

"What is it?" asked Roger.

"That's what we wondered," said Mercanton. "Go on. Look at them."

Puzzled, Roger picked up the books and leafed through

them. They were old school books, much used and filled with scribblings. He glanced up and found Marthe and Mercanton regarding him with amusement. Struck with an idea, he studied the books once more, examining the bindings. He found a bit of paper stuck in the spine of one. He pulled it out and shook the book until a small wad of franc notes fell out onto the table.

"From the Germans?" he asked. The couple laughed as delightedly as children.

"You see how clever he is," said Marthe. "It took us hours to find that. It's just like a spy film." Roger counted out ten thousand francs.

"Is that all?" he asked.

"Yes, it's not very much," said Mercanton. "Scarcely two weeks' salary. It came yesterday." Roger picked up the wrapping. It bore the sender's name and address and a Paris postmark.

"You don't know this name?" Roger asked.

"No. It's probably false," Mercanton replied. "I wouldn't have opened it if I'd known what it was. Marthe thought maybe there was a message in the books, so I read all through them. It's extraordinary what school children write in their books. Then I noticed the little piece of paper in the back and found the money."

"It's remarkable you found it at all." Roger shook his head and chuckled. "They really go in for all the trimmings, don't they?"

"Oh, we're really living a drama here," said Marthe ironically. "You see, you can't leave us for long."

"The Germans owe you money, don't they?" Roger asked, turning to the man.

"Yes, on the first of November. Charlot paid me for three months in July."

"I think we'd better ask for more when we tell them about this package." A plan was forming in Roger's mind that was to occupy much of their time in the weeks that followed, and was to have a profound effect on all their lives. But I will deal with that later.

They talked some more about the package, and then Roger said: "You know, I almost didn't come back this time. My office had a notion of putting somebody else on the job." Both Marthe and Mercanton looked at him as if they had been struck dumb. He was instantly sorry he had said anything.

"But you aren't serious," said Marthe, recovering her breath. "They couldn't do such a thing."

"No, of course not," Roger said, smiling reassuringly. It had been stupid of him to alarm them unnecessarily. Even to him, now that he was with the couple again, the idea was shocking. "It was just a possibility. I put an end to it."

"They couldn't do such a thing," Marthe repeated, still a little breathless. "The whole thing would be impossible without you."

"Don't worry. I have no intention of leaving." Roger spoke with convincing resolve.

II

THE life of Roger and the Mercantons continued to grow in security and mutual understanding. Sometimes, Roger wondered how it was possible. It required a constant avoidance of the truth. It was particularly hard for him, of course. He was as tormented as a man would be who could see into the future. But after awhile, he forced himself to believe that there might be a happy ending. It required only an easy rationalization to lead him to an active determination to assure a happy ending. But Roger had not yet gone so far. He simply allowed himself to become completely absorbed into the life of the farm. With winter approaching, there was less to do around the place. When he was not working with Mercanton, he spent much of his time with Marthe.

One day, they drove down the valley together to the little town on the hill to pass final judgment on Marthe's saint. They found her, as described, laid out in a glass case, a dark, shrunken object dressed in a nun's habit, with skin like old leather. Roger, unused to the Catholic Church, tried to create in himself the mood of reverence which he considered fitting in the presence of the curious object. Marthe, on the other hand, was determined to see all there was to see. She circled about the case, standing on tip-toe to get a better view of the corpse, pressing her face up against the glass to verify the stories about the ever-growing fingernails. In spite of himself, Roger began to laugh, trying to hold himself in. Marthe had so very much the air of a woman shopping for a good bargain. When they were outside again, Roger leaned against the side of the church and whooped with suppressed amusement.

"Well, what did you decide?" he asked when he could speak again.

"I didn't like her at all," Marthe said with finality. They walked back to the car. "She wasn't my idea of what a

saint should look like. You know, I read somewhere that
they had to cut a piece off her—well, off her back to build
up her nose after some rats ate it. I think it's dreadful to
do that to anybody."

"So now you have no saint." **Roger** started the car and
set off for home.

"I don't really mind. I could never pray to that poor
little old thing. I'm afraid I'm not very religious anyway. I
think there's too much talk about the life hereafter and not
nearly enough about the life we're leading now. Do you
believe in astrology—you know, foretelling the future?"

"Not particularly."

"Neither do I. But I went to a woman a few years ago.
She was interesting. She told me a lot of things about my
life she couldn't possibly have known. And she said that
my husband would meet a violent death in May of 1947.
I thought I might pray to that poor little saint to change
the date, just to be on the safe side. But I think it would
be more sure just to keep my husband in bed all that month.
Poor Jean Louis. I don't think he will like that."

She broke into a little song about a sailor who put to
sea without knowing how to sail. It was one of many foolish nursery songs Marthe had taught Roger and he joined
in heartily. They sang through the song twice, enjoying
the innocent words and the brief natural gaiety they felt
in each other.

"It's very strange," said Marthe when the song was
ended. "I never thought we'd be singing together when
you first came to the house—when was it? Not quite three
months ago."

"I'd just as soon forget about that day," Roger said uncomfortably. He hated to be reminded of his ambiguous position in the family.

"I'll never forget the moment you walked into the house as long as I live. I knew why you had come. I'd expected it for weeks. I felt . . . it's hard to explain. But I always knew it would happen. It was almost a relief to know it was over. And then that night, when my husband was with you in Marseille. I thought life had ended. I didn't expect to see my husband ever again. It's odd that people can suffer so much and go on living."

"I don't know. I've never suffered like that. But I should think you'd rather not talk about it."

"Yes, you seem to me one of the lucky people who haven't suffered much. And yet, you have much understanding. I never thought I'd be able to talk about these things with anyone. But, you know, it gives me great pleasure to be able to talk about them with you."

"I imagine there'll be very little we won't be able to talk about before we're through." Roger felt a thrill of satisfaction. It was good to know that Marthe was aware of his affection and sympathy.

"Before we're through?" she repeated, almost to herself. "Somehow, I can't imagine our ever being through. I don't think people can go through things like this together and ever be finished with each other."

"I think you're right," said Roger. He began to hum their little song, and soon Marthe joined in.

III

He frequently helped her in the kitchen, where together they devised ways of using the curious foods issued by the Army. One evening, wondering how they could best adapt a huge can of dehydrated cranberries to the French cuisine, Marthe led him into a discussion of Dominique, who worried them all.

"He hurts his father very much, you know," she said. "My husband has always believed in strict discipline for the children, and of course he's right for the little ones. But Dominique is beginning to have a mind of his own and his father doesn't realize it. They clash all the time. I don't blame my husband. Dominique is a very difficult boy. But I wish you could make my husband see that he doesn't handle him properly."

"That's asking a lot," said Roger. "I don't think I have the right to tell your husband how to deal with his own son."

"Oh, you know you have the right to do anything here. My husband would listen to anything you said. Besides, I think Dominique might be dangerous. He doesn't have the proper respect for his father. I know he suspects something about your work. It might be better if he knew the truth. All the children are very much against the Germans, you know. I think children are always for the winning side. I'm afraid Dominique might imagine things and try to cause trouble."

"Yes, I've been afraid of that once or twice myself. He behaved very strangely that day the American soldiers were here. But what do you think we ought to do about it?"

"I think if you talked to my husband and made him realize he must be more understanding of Dominique, things would be better. I believe Dominique thinks of his father as an enemy. Actually, my husband loves the children very much. It hurts him when Dominique opposes him. You see, my husband wants Dominique to start his training for the Navy in a year or so—as soon as he's old enough. Dominique doesn't want to. He has no aptitude for mathematics and the other things important for such a career. He doesn't know what he wants to do. He's not a clever boy, but he is sensitive. He's also stubborn, like his father."

"Don't you think it would be better for you to talk to your husband?"

"Oh, no, my friend. My husband thinks I'm too easy with the children. Perhaps I am. I have ideas of my own about education, though I wouldn't dare tell my husband. I believe in discipline, too. But when children begin to think for themselves, I believe they ought to be encouraged, even though it leads them into trouble. It's hard to see your own children make mistakes, but most people make mistakes sooner or later, anyway, so maybe it's better they should make them when they're young, when it doesn't matter so much. I was brought up very strictly. I wish I'd had a chance to learn then some of the things I'm finding out now."

"But you've had a happy life," said Roger, sensing danger in the direction the conversation was taking.

"Yes, I've had a very happy life, but I was lucky to be

married to a good man," Marthe said simply. "I've always been very much in love with my husband. It's only in the last few years that I've felt things might have been different. The last few years have been very bad for everybody. I don't think it's good for people to suffer so much."

"No, it's not good. It's wrong that it should be difficult to lead decent, peaceful lives. There's going to have to be a lot of changes in the world."

"Well, maybe it will be better soon. Maybe we'll all be able to be happy again. You will go back to America and get married and come to visit us with your wife. You will come to visit us, won't you?"

"Of course I will," said Roger. He avoided Marthe's eyes and picked up the can of cranberries. "Now, what are we going to do with this? In America, we make a sauce of it and serve it with turkey."

"But here we have no turkey. You say it's a kind of fruit? Maybe I could make a tart. What do you think?" Marthe regarded the can speculatively.

"I'm sure you could. But if it's good, you'll revolutionize the cranberry industry."

Later that evening when they were all having dinner, a chance remark of Mercanton's about the Navy reminded Roger of his conversation with Marthe and he said:

"Dominique is going into the Navy, isn't he?"

"Yes, as soon as he's old enough," said Mercanton. "I think it will be very good for him."

"We'll see about that," Dominique muttered into his plate.

"What did you say, Dominique?" Mercanton asked sharply.

"Nothing," said Dominique, lowering his head even closer to his plate.

"I want you to repeat what you said," Mercanton insisted.

"Don't you want to go into the Navy?" Roger cut in.

"I don't know." Dominique shrugged his shoulders elaborately, continuing to address his plate.

"There you are," Mercanton burst out with exasperation, "he doesn't want to do anything. He thinks he can just sit back and enjoy life. But life isn't like that. I've tried to make him realize that you have to fight for what you get. Nobody can do the things he wants and amount to anything."

"I don't know," Roger said slowly. "I think people ought to be able to do what they want."

"But that's just what happened in France," Mercanton said. "Everybody wanted to enjoy themselves. They didn't want to work. You see what happened."

"Yes, but maybe Dominique thinks he can find some work that he would enjoy, too."

"Young people shouldn't think about enjoyment. I certainly was never allowed to think of my own pleasure. Life isn't made for enjoyment. The important thing is to accomplish something. The Navy is fine training. He doesn't have to stay in it, but it would train him to accomplish something. That's what he needs. I certainly got a wonderful training in the Navy."

"Maybe after the war there won't be any Navy," Marthe suggested. "If there's going to be an international government and no more wars, we won't need a Navy."

"Don't worry. There will be more wars," said Mercan-

ton. "There always have been wars and there always will
be wars. Look at Russia. As I understand it, the Americans are already afraid of Russia."

"I'm afraid you're right," said Roger. "But I'd rather go
on hoping for awhile." He turned back to Dominique,
asking kindly: "Tell me. What would you rather do than
go into the Navy?" Dominique muttered something incomprehensible without looking up.

"You see, he can't even speak properly," his father exclaimed. "Dominique, answer the gentleman's question."

"What does it matter what I think?" the boy burst out
wildly. "You wouldn't pay any attention. All you ever
do is tell me how wonderful you are. I don't care what
happens to me. But I know things about you. And this
friend of yours, too. You just better look out, that's all.
All of you." He burst into tears and ran from the room.
The group at the table looked after him with shocked
astonishment.

"What's the matter with Dominique?" demanded little
Pierre.

"He's just a very bad boy," said Mercanton. His face
was white. He stroked Pierre's cheek with his fingers.
"You'll never be a bad boy like that, will you?" The little
boy grinned and shook his head.

"I'm sorry," Marthe said to Roger. "I'm very much
ashamed of him."

"It was all my fault," Roger said. "I'm sorry, too." He
was deeply disturbed. It was no use. They could patch
together a picture of felicity but it was, finally, a futile
effort. Their common life came apart at the seams at the
slightest stress. Now they would have to watch Dominique

day and night—three adults stalking an overwrought child. Roger wondered bitterly what psychiatry would have to say about that as an environmental influence. And what would become of the boy when Mercanton was subjected to a public trial after the war? Even the younger children were old enough to feel the destructive shock of such a disgrace. Roger sought desperately for the redeeming core of justice in a situation that demanded the payment of five lives for the error of a single individual. If it were only leading to some recognizable good. Oh sure, they were helping to win the war. But there were other ways of doing that. It wasn't enough. Maybe. . . . Yes, maybe he would have something to say about how this nasty game ended.

Mercanton pushed his chair back from the table and rose. "I'd better go up and speak to Dominique," he said.

"Yes," Roger responded heavily. "Yes, you'd better speak to him."

I V

WHENEVER he felt free to take time off, Roger ran into Cannes to see Danielle. As the strangeness wore away from their relationship, Roger quickly came to recognize the fact that he was completely in love with the girl. The rainy season had begun in earnest by that time, so they were in the habit of retreating to Roger's borrowed villa, where they would build a fire and settle into the deep chairs in the neglected drawing room, drifting into a world inhabited only by themselves. They liked to spread cushions on the floor and make love in the glow of the firelight.

It was there, at their fourth meeting, that they decided to get married. Not right away but someday, when the war was over. Roger liked less and less to talk about the future. Something in him balked at it. He no longer felt free to think of himself in terms of a postwar world. The future had become a secret, something to be avoided. And he experienced an unreasoning resentment at Danielle's natural inclination to turn the talk in that direction. This time, however, his urge to settle things with Danielle helped him to overcome this feeling. They were seated side by side in front of the fire. Danielle twisted herself around in her chair, her elbows resting on its arm, her chin cupped in her hands. She regarded Roger impishly.

"You haven't told me about your girl in the States," she said. "All you Americans are engaged to a girl at home. If you aren't already married."

Roger chuckled. "I promise you I'm not married. No, I have no girl at home."

"I don't believe you for a minute. Tell me about her."

He made a playful pass at her chin. "All right. You win. There was a sort of girl. But she doesn't mean anything to me."

"You mustn't talk like that about her. She's probably wildly in love with you. Poor girl. Are you engaged to her?"

"No, of course not. Well, that is, I was once in a way. I was brought up with her. It was one of those things." He stretched out his hand, smoothing her hair. She drew away from him, laughing at him.

"Ah, well. I see you'll have to go back and marry her.

Everybody will expect it of you. Too bad. We could have had such a lovely time together."

"Dearest, you mustn't talk like that." Roger broke through her bantering tone. "I'm going to marry you. You're going to marry me. You know that, don't you?"

"Yes, darling." She slid out of her chair and curled up at his feet, pressing her cheek against his knee. "Of course, I'm going to marry you. I'll even become an American if you want me to. Where are we going to live?"

"We can think about that later." He leaned over and tilted back her head and kissed her.

V

ROGER came frequently to see me on his trips into Cannes, keeping me posted on developments in the country and asking my advice about Danielle. I remember his telling me about their decision to get married. He spoke about it with an apologetic, almost guilty manner that I didn't like at all.

"This is such a hell of a time to talk about love and happiness," he said. "I don't feel as if I had the right to plan on the future."

"That sounds like a streak of your Puritan ancestors," I said.

"I know it does. But I don't mean it that way. I'm very happy with Danielle, and then all of a sudden I remember things—other people, and the things the war is doing to their lives. I can't help it. I try to forget the war when I'm with her, but it just doesn't work."

I think Danielle was more disturbed by this feeling in

Roger than she liked to admit to herself. I met her in the street the day after one of his visits and we inevitably spoke of him.

"You certainly found me a prima donna," she said with a rueful little smile. "I think maybe you should have left him on that LST."

"I've been wondering whether I oughn't to speak to you about that," I said. "Are you sure you're wise to count on him so completely? I'm afraid he's pretty mixed up inside."

She immediately sprang to his defense. "I was just joking. He's a very wonderful person. It's just that people are affected by the war in funny ways. He's a little difficult sometimes. But I can understand that. If anything important were involved, he could never fail me. We've found something very precious together. It's something nobody else can understand, I suppose. We mean everything to each other."

As we talked, she unintentionally revealed her whole feeling towards Roger. Like most Europeans, she had suffered too much to let the war interfere with the possibility of her own happiness. She had had to harden herself to the misery of others. She felt she had the right to think of herself. She frankly wanted Roger, and the morbid hesitations she felt in him confused and tormented her. She could never have understood his confining absorption in his job, his innocent struggle to give it an ethical direction. She shared the European heritage of war. One fought, first on one side and then the other, in a constant effort for survival. Meanwhile, one found as much in life as possible. The war was over for her, its issues had long since been resolved. Her feeling for Roger was the reward for the agony of the past few years.

There was little I could say to either of them. I could simply hope that the strength of their feeling for each other would carry them through to the end of the war, when they could escape the conflict of external pressures.

VI

Towards the end of December, Roger looked me up at my office. He wanted me to help him with his Christmas shopping for the family in the country. I knew most of the local shopkeepers well enough to have access to the secret stock they kept hidden for the privileged. Accompanying Roger from shop to shop, I was touched by the care with which he made his selections from the meager supply of books and toys. He was plainly determined to make the most of this Christmas. He tried out all the toys himself, solemnly asking my advice about the merits of this one or that. When he was finished, he had an impressive load of gifts.

"Nothing for the parents?" I asked when we had completed the round of the toy shops.

"No. We've decided not to give each other anything. Too difficult to find things worth having."

"I take it you won't be here for Christmas."

"No. I'll stay out in the country."

We wished each other season's greeting and he drove away.

At the farm, the whole family was busy with preparations for the holiday. It was the first Christmas in four years that the French had spent in freedom. Although the news was not encouraging, there was a conviction that this would be the last Christmas of war. Mercanton devoted himself to fattening up the choicest of his rabbits. Roger had promised them a turkey from his headquarters in Marseille. Marthe spent much of her day with her chickens, cheering them on to greater production so that there would be plenty of eggs for the Christmas cake. When Roger arrived with the presents for the children, they all three locked themselves in the living room while Roger displayed his marvels.

"But they're breath-taking," said Marthe. "You'll always be Santa Claus to the children now."

"Oh, they mustn't all be from me," Roger said. "They'll be from all of us." He and Mercanton settled themselves on the floor, winding up the mechanical trucks and firing toy cannon at each other.

"You know," said Mercanton, studying the cannon, "I think if I mounted a small bar here and ran a wire back from the rod I could increase the power of these guns."

Roger took aim and released a pellet that landed squarely on Mercanton's head.

"Bravo, bravo," Marthe cried. "I don't think the children will have a chance with these toys." They fired several more shots at each other, laughing and boasting of their prowess, though Roger scored most of the hits.

"I think you'd better surrender, Jean Louis," Marthe said. "He's a dangerous man."

"You know, I think we ought to have a real holiday," Roger said. "Why don't we tell our friends you're having your family stay with you and you can't work for a few days?"

"Good," Mercanton agreed. "If you don't mind, I think I ought to send Christmas greetings to them."

"That's fine. I meant to mention it myself." So Roger and Mercanton put aside the toys, while they composed a message of Christmas cheer to the Germans, wishing them a happy New Year, and adding that for a day or two at Christmas time Mercanton would not transmit. The day after they sent it they received a similar message from the other side, wishing Mercanton and his family all holiday cheer.

"You know, I'm growing rather fond of Blum," Roger said while they were decoding the message. "He plays with us so nicely."

VII

THEY decided to make the presentation of gifts to the children on Christmas Eve. They had a fine dinner that night, though it was only a mild preparation for the feast that was to come the next day. The children were in a fever of anticipation. The two younger ones couldn't remember a Christmas of such carefree delight. Dominique, too, was child enough to be excited by the promise of wonders contained in the hints of the adults. Roger and the Mercantons continued to regard him as a threat, and they did all they could to coax him into the prevailing holiday mood. For the moment, they felt they had succeeded. So they all laughed together, and told jokes on each other, the oft-repeated, intimate jokes of close family association, and felt secure and at peace.

Roger was captivated by the atmosphere, remembering other Christmases long ago in the big house in Sixty-fifth Street, when life seemed to shimmer with breathless enchantment. He remembered the smell of spices and strong drink, the after-breakfast rush for the tree buttressed with mounds of packages in fabulous wrappings, and the snow piled on the sidewalks, to get dirty so quickly; and he remembered when he was very little, a fine big sleigh with his father, handsome and a trifle self-conscious, holding the jingling reins. They were pleasant memories, but without any binding sentiment. The family life he had known had been expensive but rather chill. He was grateful to these people for evoking the past, revivifying it, joining it to the present in a warm glow of affection.

When dinner was finished they all went into the living room where the presents were laid beside the crèche which Marthe had prepared with great care—an odd and amusing procession of Biblical and Provençal figures, winding through sprigs of trees to the brightly lighted manger. For awhile, the room was a confusion of wrappings and the excited cries of the children. In spite of their agreement, there was a package for Roger from Marthe—a sweater and a pair of wool socks.

"That's not really a present," Marthe explained. "It's a precaution. We've got to take care of you. What would happen to all of us if you were to get sick?"

"But where did you find all the wool?" Roger asked, knowing that it was unobtainable in the shops.

"I have a confession. It's not new. I had to take apart some old things of mine. I think they turned out very well, considering."

Later, when the presents had all been opened and the excitement had somewhat subsided, they turned on the radio to a program of Christmas carols and all joined in singing the familiar words. Roger and Marthe harmonized together, vying with one another to achieve startling effects. In their exuberance, they sometimes went very wrong, and then they all broke down and laughed until the tears came. When it was time for the children to go to bed, they formed a procession led by Mercanton carrying the baby, Françoise, on his back, and sang their way up to the children's room. Afterwards, Roger and Marthe and Mercanton returned to the living room and sat for awhile drinking some brandy that Roger had brought from Cannes.

"I haven't had so much fun for years," Marthe sighed contentedly.

"This is very fine brandy," said Mercanton. "It was kind of you to bring it."

"Very kind," Marthe said thoughtfully. "You have been very kind. You've given us all a very happy Christmas."

"And you've made my Christmas very happy, too, so I think we're even," Roger said lightly.

"No, we owe everything to you," Marthe went on slowly. "I often think what it would have been like if it had been someone else. You've made everything possible, and we'll never forget it. I want you to know we're very grateful. Heaven knows what would have become of us if it had been someone else. My husband doesn't like to talk about these things, but I know he feels the same way."

"I think Roger knows these things without our saying them," Mercanton said hurriedly, a note of annoyance hiding his embarrassment. Roger felt his throat contract and his eyes were hot. Too much brandy, he thought to himself angrily.

"Sure. Let's not be so solemn. Let's drink to us," he said. He spoke with difficulty, feeling the words catch.

"And to another Christmas together?" Marthe said, raising her glass. Roger drank down his brandy, glad for the heat that brought tears to his eyes.

CHAPTER
Eight

ʃʃ

I

THE arrival of the money concealed in the package of books had given Roger an idea. After Christmas, his interest in the radio transmissions became more and more intense as it became apparent that his notion might be successful. He had persuaded himself that if Mercanton contributed a striking service to the war effort, he might receive more lenient treatment when his job was done.

Accordingly, he had instructed Mercanton to demand more money when acknowledging receipt of the books. The Germans had asked him to wait until after Christmas, when they would put him in touch with an agent in Nice who would, by that time, be supplied with funds. At Roger's suggestion, Mercanton refused to make a personal contact, pointing out the dangers involved. He proposed, instead, that the contact be made by a cousin who was absolutely trustworthy and might be useful for other jobs. Roger had won permission from his headquarters to play this role. After a good many questions, the Germans consented, and promised to forward details of the rendezvous later.

Now, Roger ordered Mercanton to reopen the subject.

It was agreed that Roger was to make friends with the agent in Nice so that, as time passed, he might learn the names of those working for the Germans in that area. There were to be no arrests until Roger felt he had penetrated the organization as thoroughly as possible. Roger was well satisfied. If all went well, he and Mercanton might be responsible for closing up all the leaks of information through the Franco-Italian border.

All through the first weeks of the new year, the affair hung fire. Then one day in the last week of January, Mercanton received orders that were characteristically abrupt. His cousin was to meet a man named Paul the following night in Nice at the Café des Quatre Reines. A time was specified and a password given. Paul had been instructed to hand over the sum of one hundred thousand francs. It was hoped that Mercanton would consider this sufficient payment for his loyalty and patience. A brief description of Paul followed.

Alight with satisfaction and anticipation, Roger drove immediately into Aix. This promised to be a fascinating adventure. But more than that, it might be the solution to the Mercanton case he had been looking for. A coup of the sort he was planning would surely count in the Frenchman's favor.

He telephoned the information into his headquarters, using his system of double-talk, and by the same means, was informed that Meddling was out of town for several days but would be contacted as soon as possible. The next day, Roger was ready to leave shortly after lunch. He had made a careful check of his pockets and the car to see that he was carrying nothing that would reveal his identity.

He had decided to leave even his special papers behind him. Mercanton was to do nothing until Roger's return. He and Marthe accompanied Roger to the car.

"You will take care of yourself," Marthe said as Roger started the motor. She didn't know the details of the project, but she felt that this was a special occasion. "Take care of yourself," she repeated. "We'll be waiting for you." She and Mercanton stood in the drive and waved as Roger drove away.

He had left early so that there would be time to see Danielle before going on to Nice. But military traffic was heavy on the road, and he was already well behind schedule when, just past Frejus, entering the Esterels, he was forced to pull over to the side of the road and stop altogether. A long military convoy was coming through from the direction of Nice. Automatically, he began counting the trucks as they passed, making a note of their types and markings. They roared by in apparently endless procession, making the air tremble with their might, each loaded with mathematical precision, each a symbol of some law of mechanical perfection, even to the two soldiers installed, like part of the machinery, in each cab. Suddenly punctuating the line, a French unit straggled by, their trucks garlanded in early mimosa, the French soldiers lolling in any available space, roaring a war-like song into the early evening. Despite his impatience, Roger was struck by the sudden burst of humanity that erupted defiantly out of the bleak mechanical stream. It seemed a reassertion of man's ability to shape his environment to the pattern of his own desire. Roger glanced at his watch for the hundredth time. He couldn't reach Cannes now before seven o'clock. His appointment in Nice was for ten. He would have little time for Danielle. He wondered with annoyance whether he ought to give up seeing her this evening. The last truck finally rumbled past and he threw his car into gear, racing forward to make up for lost time.

When he reached Danielle's home, the girl was out. He agreed to wait a few minutes, and was shown by the maid into a small study. There he paced about impatiently, fidgeting with his watch and rehearsing in his mind the evening's work. He would wait only ten more minutes, he decided. Although Nice was less than an hour away, he should leave time for mishaps on the road. He could take no chances with his plan. Everything depended on it. What in the world could Danielle be doing? You'd suppose she'd make an effort to stay near home. She knew he might turn up at any time. He was about to leave, when Danielle came hurrying into the room, her face bright with pleasure at seeing him again.

"Oh, darling, it's so wonderful to see you," she said, running to him. "Where've you been all year? There's so much I want to tell you."

"I'm afraid it'll have to wait," Roger said, on edge with disappointment at having so little time with her. "I have work to do. I've been waiting for you for half an hour."

"I know. It's so awful not knowing when you might turn up. I've got in the habit of just hanging about the house all day on the chance that you might come. My family thinks I'm having some sort of breakdown." She laughed. "Maybe I am. It is a little insane to miss you so much." She put her arms against his chest and kissed him.

"I wish you'd arrived sooner," said Roger. He felt each

minute passing now, preoccupation with the business ahead of him crowding out all other thought. "I really must leave."

"But you'll be around for a few days?"

"I don't know. I've some very important work to do. I won't be able to make any plans until it's finished." He spoke with thoughtless brusqueness.

"But I will see you soon?" She tried to ignore the rebuff. How long must she be patient? Why must he always make it so difficult for her?

"Darling, I tell you I don't know. I never know when I'm going to be free. You know that." Roger fell automatically into evasion.

"But don't you understand? I must talk to you about something." Her voice was growing urgent.

"It'll have to wait," Roger said carelessly. He looked at his watch once more. "I must go now."

"But you can't go," Danielle cried violently. Roger stood uncertainly before her, astonished by her manner. "You've got to listen to me. I'm going to have a baby." Her words came out in a rush.

Roger started at her for a moment, trying to absorb what she had said. She made a slight movement towards him, and then was still, waiting for him to acknowledge her. He turned from her abruptly.

"Oh, for Christ's sake," he muttered roughly.

"You're angry." Her tone was almost incredulous. Here at last was the test. She was suddenly overcome with panic. What if he should fail her now? There would be nothing left for her. She had given him all her faith. She had given herself joyously, never doubting him for a moment. She couldn't bear to admit the possibility that she might have been wrong.

"I'm not angry. But, good God, what do you expect me to feel?" His mind was in a turmoil. He didn't have time to think about this now.

"I thought you might possibly be glad," she said faintly. She could feel a chill gripping her, striking deep within her.

"How can I be glad?" he broke out. "This is no time for that sort of thing. You'll have to do something about it."

She faced him, feeling as if she were seeing him from a great distance. "I can't. It's too late. It happened that first time I met you. Besides, I wouldn't. I wanted to have it."

"You must be out of your mind," he said brutally. "Don't you see it would be all wrong now?" He realized quickly that he must alter his manner if he were to get away. He approached her, assuming a gentleness calculated to soothe her.

"Look, I'll try to see you tomorrow. I'm sure I'll be able to. We'll try to figure something out."

She drew away. She didn't want his sympathy. She wanted a life with him in which they both shared equally. If he couldn't meet this situation with an honest sense of participation, then nothing was worthwhile, nothing mattered. She must think clearly. She must try to face it. She made an effort to still the mounting terror within her.

"There's nothing to figure out. I've loved you, and you told me you loved me." She felt indignation and heartbroken disappointment forcing through her control. "I've never tried to conceal how I feel about you. I've given myself completely to you. Do you think that gives you the right to use me in any way you choose? A minute ago you were so busy you didn't know when you could see me again. That's why I told you. I wanted you to know. Now, all of a sudden, you can see me tomorrow—'to figure things out.' You talk a lot about honesty and your duty to mankind. It sounds wonderful. But when are you going to apply your fine principles to life?"

"Now, look here. You know very well I have obligations that come before anything else." He was in no mood for a scene. He glanced quickly at his watch.

"Oh, the war," she said mockingly. She was too hurt to care what she said. "I know all about the war. I've fought it, too—a lot longer than you have. You Americans think we should be so grateful to you for fighting that we shouldn't ask for anything more. Well, I expected a lot more. If you had all these obligations, why did you take me in the first place? Was that honest? You knew what it meant to me. No, you liked having a girl to go to bed with, and whenever it got in your way, you could have other obligations." She was horrified as she heard herself accuse him. Was that really the way it had been?

"Goddammit, I'm going. You can think what you like." Roger was furious. He didn't like it any better than she did. But it wasn't fair to reproach him for a situation that was beyond his control. "I'll see you when I can." He turned and stamped out of the room.

She stood without moving, scarcely aware that he was gone. This couldn't have happened. She had been so happy about the baby. She could have gone through anything with Roger. You can think what you like. What you

like. That's what he said. Everybody could do and think
what they liked. Nobody cared. It made everything so
much simpler. Of course he didn't want their child. How
careless of her to have a child. The joke was on her. Hilari-
ous. She was an Unmarried Mother. There were institu-
tions that would take care of her. So amusing. She fought
the icy hysteria rising within her. She had been through
too much. Her reserves were exhausted. She wanted to
hide herself away from the world. She felt the need for
a dark protection. She walked slowly from the room and
mounted the stairs. She was possessed by the terror.

I I

ROGER reached Nice with an hour to spare. He located
the Café des Quatre Reines up a narrow street in the old
part of town, and then drove to the Promenade des Anglais.
He left his car and walked. He was trying to keep his mind
clear for the impending meeting, but his thoughts kept
slipping back to Danielle. What a hell of a situation. She
must have known about it when he saw her last. Why
hadn't she told him then, when they still could have done
something about it? He wished he could make her understand how he felt. He believed in their happiness together.
But he wanted to wait until he was free. All the same . . .
she was bearing his child. A sudden surprising surge of
pride passed over him. His child. Well, maybe they'd be
able to work something out. He would see her tomorrow
and they would talk about it.

He drove back to the old town and parked his car
around the corner from the cafe. It was a few minutes

to ten. He had trouble finding the entrance because of the blackout and the narrow streets which shut out all light from the sky. When he came upon the small sign advertising the café, he went in and heard voices coming from the floor above. He climbed a long flight of stairs and passed through a door on the left of the hallway.

He found himself in a big, bare, brightly lighted room, with a bar at one end and tables placed along the walls. It took him an instant to realize that there were no women in the place, and that everybody at the bar had turned to look at him as he stood hesitating at the door. Music was coming from the next room and, looking in that direction, he saw several men dancing together. He turned back to the bar and found the row of eyes still on him—the eyes of boys with prettily waving hair and finely arched eyebrows. As he glanced down the row, several of them smiled at him invitingly. He turned hastily away and sought a table in the corner. Before he had reached it, he felt a hand on his arm, and as he drew back he heard a voice say:

"Excuse me. Are you M. Dulin?" Roger turned and found a short, middle-aged man beside him, stout but solid-looking, with a broad face, narrow eyes and a close-clipped mustache. He matched the description Roger had received the day before. His clothes were shabby but he wore them neatly. He looked to Roger like a modest business man, except that there was an air of hardiness about him, as if he were accustomed to working out of doors. An engineer, possibly, or a sailor.

"You are M. Paul?" Roger asked.

"Yes. It's very cool out tonight." The man kept his sharp little eyes on Roger as he spoke.

"Yes," said Roger, carefully following instructions. "But not so cool as it was in 1939."

"Umm. Yes." The man gave a brief little nod. "Now that we've got that over with, I think we can sit down. That's the silliest line I ever heard." They sat down at a secluded table in the corner and called a waiter.

"Two brandies. That will do?" The man gave the order and waved the waiter away. "Why our friends think that grown men have to go through that sort of nonsense, I will never understand. You are obviously M. Dulin. I am plainly M. Paul. That should be enough." The man popped his eyes in a way that was apparently a nervous mannerism and remained silent until the brandy was put in front of him. He took a quick gulp from his glass and spoke again. "Well, M. Dulin, what do you think of our meeting place?"

"I don't like it very much."

"You find it disgusting? Of course. That's why we're safe here. Nobody here dares inquire into his neighbor's business. Corruption shields corruption. Vice hides behind vice. Every place else in Nice is crawling with agents and informers of every possible description." He took another quick sip of his brandy and popped his eyes. He turned and studied Roger closely.

"You know, M. Dulin, there's something about you— I'm not sure. You seem to me like a very nice young man. I'm not sure I like that."

"I've found it a great asset in this business."

"Possibly. Well, M. Dulin, let's talk business. I don't like to stay in this place too long. I find the atmosphere grows a bit rich." The rooms were filling up. Shrill voices

called to each other. Roger noticed a sprinkling of uniforms in the crowd. He had to lean close to M. Paul to
hear him above the blare of the music. The dancing
couples were spreading out from the next room into the
bar. As they glided by, they looked over their partners'
shoulders to cast long provocative glances at Roger. As
one boy whirled past, M. Paul looked up and winked
lewdly at him. He turned to Roger.

"Ridiculous, isn't it? But one must keep up appearances.
I don't think you ought to try it, though, unless you want
the whole lot on your lap. Well, then. I'm informed that
you will be available for various jobs under my direction.
If we're to continue our association, you will have to know
my name and address. Before I give them to you, however,
I'll have to warn you to consider them strictly confiden-
tial." As M. Paul spoke, Roger became aware of a com-
motion over by the door. Four young men came spilling
into the room, giggling and pushing. In their midst, being
led by the hand, was George Meddling.

A shock passed through Roger at seeing him here. Had
something gone wrong at headquarters? Then some sly
gossip about Meddling's past flashed through his mind. So
that was the way things were. He turned away quickly,
but as he did so, Meddling caught his eye. He heard him
call "Rog" from across the room, and in a moment he was
beside the table, weaving slightly and laughing uproar-
iously.

"Well, well, if it isn't old Rog," he said. "I'm a little
drunk. How's old Rog? A little drunk too, old Rog?"

"Sure, I'm a little drunk too, Major," Roger said, hoping
Meddling would take warning at the unfamiliar title.

"Major! Why so formal? What's old Rog doing so far from home?"

"Just taking a little trip, Major," Roger persisted.

"Well, that's great," Meddling said enthusiastically. "Glad to see you. I want to talk to you."

"Fine. I'll look in on you some time," said Roger, terrified of what might come next.

"Damned decent of you," Meddling said with elaborate satire. "Imagine finding old Rog in this place. I think you're embarrassed. Mustn't be embarrassed, Rog. Boys will be boys, you know."

"Sure. Look, I'll talk to you later," said Roger with desperation.

"Don't worry. I don't want to break anything up. But we should've gotten together sooner, Rog. Come on over to the table if you get a chance. I want you to meet the kids."

"Fine. I'll do that," Roger replied, filled with revulsion. Meddling leaned over and patted him on the back, then wandered off to join his friends. Roger took a quick drink of brandy, giving himself time to compose himself. M. Paul had watched the brief encounter with close attention.

"I see you speak excellent English, M. Dulin," he said. "You didn't tell me you were on such good terms with the Americans."

"I have some friends," Roger said, attempting a casual note.

"But do they stay your friends when you treat them like that? I should think a—what was he?—a major in the American Army might be very useful. If you work for me, I should want you to be more cordial."

"I don't like that man. He's very tiresome."

"I see. Even though he might bring you in a little extra money? You know, M. Dulin, I'm afraid I was right. You're a very nice young man."

"I don't let it interfere with my work. What were we talking about? You want me to have your address? When do you want me to contact you again?"

"I've been thinking it over. I don't think that will be necessary right now. I think possibly it would be better if we met here again in a week or so."

"Just as you wish. You name the day."

"Let's say a week from tomorrow, at the same time."

"Fine. Now, what about the money?"

"The money? You know, I've just realized I've forgotten the money," M. Paul said blandly. "I do that sort of thing all the time. I'm afraid you'll find it an annoying trait. I'll surely bring it with me next time."

Roger had only a second to make up his mind. This man had been put on his guard. If his suspicions were concerned entirely with Roger's competence, only the opportunity to penetrate his activities had been lost. But if they went further than that, so that he might cast a doubt on Mercanton's authenticity, all the painstaking labor of the past five months would be wasted. Roger made his decision. He slipped his hand into his coat and drew his .45 part way from its shoulder holster.

"M. Paul, I don't want you to move," he said, keeping his voice friendly. "From where you're sitting, I want to show you something." He drew his jacket back slightly, revealing the gun. "Now then. I promise you I'm not afraid to use it. We'll walk quietly out of here and continue our talk outside."

"I see I was mistaken about you," the stocky little man said without changing his expression. "You're a very foolish young man."

"That may be. Shall we go?" He threw some money on the table and waited while the older man rose. With Roger walking a step or two behind, they crossed the floor and went out the door. Meddling, seated at a table near the door, saw them go. He sprang up and followed them in great good spirits. Roger heard him clattering down the stairs behind him.

"Hey, Rog, wait for baby," Meddling cried as he caught up to the pair at the foot of the stairs. "You can't run out on me like that. You've got to have a drink with the kids."

"Why don't you clear out?" Roger said angrily. "You've caused enough trouble already." He stood a few feet behind his prisoner, his hand still held inside his jacket. He didn't look at Meddling.

"What in hell's the matter with you?" Meddling looked from Roger to the Frenchman. "Is this . . . You mean, this is the guy . . ."

"Yes, this is the guy," Roger interrupted savagely. "A hell of a lot of use he is now."

"Why didn't you let me know about this?" Meddling was getting angry too, whipped by Roger's manner.

"I telephoned the information yesterday. If you kept in touch with the office, you'd have known about it."

"I see. I've been very busy . . ." Meddling said lamely.

"Goddammit, we can't go on talking here. If you're sober enough, you can help. My car's around the corner.

I'm going out there with this guy now. You can follow in a few minutes. But for Christ's sake, if you see anybody hanging around, stay away. This guy might have some of his friends with him." Roger turned and gestured the Frenchman to the door, leaving Meddling in the vestibule. They went out and around the corner and found the car gleaming dully in the dark. As far as Roger could see, the streets were empty.

"Open the doors, both of them," Roger ordered, standing out of reach of the Frenchman. "Now get in back." Roger slipped quickly into the front seat and turned, holding his gun out now, full on the shape in the back seat. It was too dark to see M. Paul's features, but his voice was as firm and brisk as ever when he spoke.

"I don't quite understand your game," he said. "But if it's the money you want, take it and let's move along. I could even include a small bonus. Of course, if you're working for the Americans, I suppose there's nothing to discuss." Roger knew the type. The man had lived so close to danger that now, faced with serious trouble, he wasn't touched by it.

"No, there's nothing to discuss," Roger answered him. "You should have given me the money in the first place."

"Perhaps you're right. I'm growing too old for this business. I become suspicious too easily. I gather I'm to have a vacation now?"

"Yes, you'll have a vacation," said Roger. He heard footsteps approaching the car and his fingers tightened on the gun preparing for trouble. But it was Meddling. He recognized his broad outline as he stopped beside the car.

"Come around to the driver's seat," Roger said quietly,

keeping his attention fixed on the man in back. When Meddling had installed himself behind the wheel, Roger instructed him to start the car and drive off. "That is, if you're sober enough," he added coldly.

"OK, Roger. That's enough of that. You might tell me what this is all about." He was sobering up now.

"It seems pretty clear to me. By pulling your little drunk act in there, you blew the whole deal."

"I didn't say anything in there that would blow any deal."

"You don't think so? You said enough for him to refuse to give me the money. He was suspicious enough to want a week to think the whole thing over."

"Well, so what? Why did you pull a gun on him?"

"Christ, are you crazy? I was supposed to just let him go home and tell his bosses that I looked like a phony, and so probably our friend out in the country was a phony, too?"

"Now we're getting somewhere. You mean, you were so afraid something might happen to your little pal in the country that you decided to call the whole thing off."

"You're damn right. You think I was going to let this guy go, and run the risk of blowing the works at the farm? I suppose it occurs to you that this guy might have a radio, too. He could tell the Germans everything that happened tonight."

"So what? You had orders not to make any arrests until you had the works on this guy."

"Now wait a minute. You don't mean to suggest that this bird is more important than the show in the country. It was a question of choosing between one or the other."

"You had your orders," Meddling repeated fretfully. "You should've stuck to them."

"You haven't answered my question. You know, if there's any doubt in your mind, we can put the whole thing up to Paris." There was a threat in Roger's voice.

"You'd better watch your step, Chandler." Meddling's voice was suddenly menacing. He liked Roger. He liked all his colleagues. He believed in maintaining friendly relations with them. But his deep-rooted sense of insecurity could drive him to any unscrupulous limit when he felt his own position threatened. His shrewd instinct for self-preservation was aroused now. "I've tried to be patient with you. But if you want to play dirty, I think I can match you."

"I'm sure of it. But you don't frighten me, Major."

"That's good. But you know, I think you're getting stale on this job. You're getting too wrapped up in it. I think a change would do you good. I'm very understanding, but I don't think some people would like your disobeying orders."

"Now listen, Meddling. Get this straight. I'm handling this job my way from now on. You almost wrecked the the whole thing tonight. I'm not going to give you another chance. I'm fed up with the way you work. I've built up the whole thing myself, and from now on I don't want to be interfered with."

"That's pretty big talk, Chandler. I think you'll be sorry for it."

"I don't. You're forgetting something. I don't like to work with fairies." His contempt cut through his words. He would dispose of Meddling, once and for all. "A lot of people feel the same way. If I have any trouble with you, I'll make a complete report on your behavior to-night. You know what that would mean, Major. Now, I don't want to talk about it any more. I'm sore enough already. I don't want to lose my temper."

"No, I'd hate to see you lose your temper, Roger," Meddling said with a sneer. He was frightened but he wasn't going to give Roger the satisfaction of showing it. He would let the matter drop for the time being. But he wouldn't forget it. He went on evenly: "What do you want to do with this guy?"

"We'll have to put him out of the way. We'd better leave him with the MP's here until you can take him to Marseille and give him a going over." Meddling turned several corners in silence and drew up in front of the Nice Military Police headquarters.

"You'll have to go in and make the arrangements," Roger said. He had sat all the while twisted around in his seat so that he faced the man in back. "I'll search him while you're gone."

When Meddling had left, he said: "Very well. Please hand me everything you have in your pockets. You better start with your gun."

"I am a peaceable man, monsieur," M. Paul said. "I don't carry a gun." He handed across a long envelope which, a glance told Roger, contained the money. He fumbled in his pockets and produced a half dozen identity cards, an address book, a handful of small change, a half-empty package of cigarettes and a few creased slips of paper.

In a few minutes, Meddling was back with two soldiers. Roger got out of the car and handed his gun to Meddling.

He opened the back door and helped his prisoner out. He held him for a moment in the dark street, going quickly through his pockets to make sure that nothing had been overlooked, then stepped back and allowed Meddling to take charge.

"Just put him somewhere where nobody will see him. I'll stop by for him tomorrow," Meddling said, and the two soldiers hurried the man into a side entrance.

"Well, that's that," said Meddling. "How are you going to cover this with your people?"

"Don't you worry about that. I'll just tell them the guy never showed up for his appointment." Roger walked around and got into the driver's seat. "You want to go any place?"

"I left my car back at that joint." Meddling got into the car and they drove back to the Café des Quatre Reines. As Meddling was leaving, Roger said:

"Here, you'd better take all these papers. Here's the money. There ought to be a hundred thousand francs. God knows what he was doing with all these identity cards. You'd better try to get it out of him."

"Thanks, Chandler, but there're a few things I can handle without your help." Meddling gathered up the papers and disappeared into the dark.

Roger was tired. The evening's work had taken little more than an hour, but the clash with Meddling had put him under a double strain. Driving back to Cannes, he wondered whether he should send in a report on his chief. Men like that oughtn't to be allowed in the Army. But no. He would wait. It would serve as a useful club to keep him in line. He was bitterly disappointed that his plan had so quickly gone awry. Well, something might be salvaged from it. He would have to try again. But when he considered how nearly the whole Mercanton affair had come to being wrecked, he found himself getting angry all over again. Damned irresponsibility. It wasn't just the case. There was the whole family to think of, too. That was the last time he'd bother to consult with Meddling. It was just as well the break had come. It gave him a free hand.

III

HE WAS up early the next morning, eager to see Danielle. He felt almost as if their conversation the day before hadn't taken place. He had been too preoccupied to react to her news. Now he felt refreshed and happy, cleansed by his showdown with Meddling.

So he was going to be a father. He looked at himself in the mirror as he was shaving and laughed. God knows how they'd work it all out. Maybe Danielle would have some ideas. Anyway, the war couldn't last forever. He hurried through his breakfast, seated in front of a big window looking out over the gentle sea. Maybe he could arrange to stay on here after the war. He could hardly get Danielle back to the States for a long time. Of course, later on, he would tell her about the family, and take her to see Marthe. Or would he? He skirted painfully around the thought.

Danielle. She was pretty wonderful to go through with it so unquestioningly. Maybe they could get married soon. He'd have to take it up with the Army authorities . . . Oh, they'd work things out somehow. They were in love with each other. Nothing else mattered. He was smiling foolishly to himself as he went out and got into the car. He began to sing at the top of his voice as he drove out to her house. Everything always seemed so simple after a good night's sleep. What if they did have a little bastard? It would serve his family right. He laughed out loud at the thought.

When he reached his destination he learned what I had known since the night before: he would not see her again. She had shot herself through the head.

I was just finishing breakfast when Roger arrived at my house that morning. He came in, grey, and trembling from head to foot. I was not pleased to see him.

Danielle's death had been a terrible shock to me, and I had been up late with her family. It had been a grim session. Why? The family had kept asking, almost as if disapproval were overshadowing their grief. Why? Why? As if the answer to that question would make everything all right. They asked a lot about Roger, and it was apparent that Danielle had not discussed him with them. I presumed that they knew nothing of Danielle's pregnancy. None of us mentioned it. They did tell me meaningfully that he had seen her that evening, and though I knew Roger too well to condemn him, it was clear what they were hinting at. So I shrugged aside all knowledge of him as tactfully as possible.

He just stood in the middle of the living room where I was sitting, looking through me with his large shadowed eyes, working his mouth and occasionally making broken little gasping sounds.

"I know," I said. "You'd better sit down." He turned

and slumped down in a chair and gripped his head in his hands. We sat there in silence for a long time. Occasionally his body was constricted by a racking shudder. Finally, when he seemed to have himself under control, he lay back and looked up at the ceiling.

"I'm sorry," he muttered indistinctly.

"How about a drink?" I said.

"Sure, that'd be fine." He continued to stare at the ceiling. I got up and poured us both some brandy and sat down again opposite him.

"You saw her last night?" I asked. He nodded and covered his face with his hands once more. "She told you?" I persisted. He sat forward and looked at me.

"About the baby? You knew about it?"

"Yes, I knew about it," I said. He made a helpless gesture and then I saw him drawing his body together as if he were going to spring up.

"I wish I could say something." He flung the words out. "Why do people always feel they have to say something?"

"It helps take their minds off their troubles," I said. "But if you expect me to say something reassuring, I'm afraid I'm going to disappoint you. I don't feel very much like making it easy for you, Roger. I've known Danielle since she was a little girl. She didn't frighten easily."

"No, I know." His voice was a shadow of agony. His eyes widened slowly, fixed blankly ahead of him, as he sat looking in upon himself. He seemed to recall himself after a bit, and he sat back in his chair.

"God, I'm sick of it," he said. "Cheat, combat, kill. People can't even love without hurting each other."

"They can try," I said. "The fault doesn't lie in human nature, but in what we've allowed to happen to ourselves. It's easy to feel sorry for yourself and say, 'That's life. I'm sick of it.' Every sensitive man is sick of it, but that doesn't give him the right to run away from it."

"A hell of a chance I have to run away from anything. What do you want me to think about Danielle? That it's my fault? That it's her fault? What difference does it make? We were just a couple of innocent bystanders. There're plenty of innocent bystanders. And by God, if I can, I'm going to see that some of them get a break."

"Take care, Roger. You're wrong you know. There are very few innocents in the world."

"I don't agree with you. Oh, hell, it doesn't do any good to talk about it. I've got to get back to work. Thanks for letting me sit here." He had spoken with a kind of ecstatic violence that I didn't like. He seemed to vibrate with a barely controlled, intense excitement. His mood disturbed me and I was anxious to be alone anyway, so I watched him go with a certain amount of satisfaction. Afterwards, I was sorry I hadn't encouraged him to talk more of the thoughts that were taking possession of his mind.

IV

WHEN Roger reached the farm that afternoon, the Mercantons were shocked by his appearance. He responded with difficulty to their customary happy greeting. They led him solicitously into the living room.

"Is anything the matter?" Mercanton inquired.

"No, everything's all right. I've had a tiring trip."

"Just a moment. I'll get you some wine," Marthe said. "You can rest now." She hurried off and came back with biscuits and a bottle of wine. "There. Drink that. You try to do too much. I'll have to be more strict with you."

"And you got the money all right?" Mercanton asked.

"Yes, I got the money. But I had a little trouble. To-morrow, we'll have to report that M. Paul failed to keep his appointment with your cousin." M. Paul. The money. How difficult it was to keep it all straight. Could they see there was a pain cutting into his soul that made it almost impossible to speak?

"You mean . . ." Mercanton's face was grave. "You mean, the man got away?"

"No. Everything's all right. We just can't follow the original plan, that's all." Hang on. He must hang on until these explanations were out of the way. He couldn't cry out: "What difference does it make? I don't give a damn about this lousy business." It would frighten them. Above all, Mercanton must not be upset. It might show in his work.

"You don't think the Germans will have any suspicions of me?"

"No, of course not. That's why we have to say that your cousin never made contact with M. Paul. He won't be connected with you in any way."

"That's good. It would be too bad for anything to go wrong now, after all we've done."

"What would happen if something did go wrong?" Marthe asked with concern. "I mean, suppose something happened that wasn't my husband's fault at all. What would you do then?"

What was she saying? If something went wrong? Oh God, something had gone wrong. Why hadn't he said, "It's all right. I haven't time now. But everything is all right." That's all he need have said. She had died thinking he didn't care. He clenched his fists and lifted his head.

"Don't worry," he said grimly. "I'm going to make very sure that nothing does happen."

"I somehow feel we're in good hands," said Marthe, the anxiety gone from her voice.

"Did the man really have a hundred thousand francs for us?" Mercanton asked.

"Yes, he had it all right."

"That's quite a sum," Mercanton said appreciatively. "But, tell me, if you aren't supposed to have had your appointment, how am I to have received the money?"

"You haven't. We'll have to start all over again asking for it."

"Come, Jean Louis, don't talk about that now," said Marthe. "Roger is tired. Let him rest. Here are the papers, if you want to read." She handed Roger several of the small handbills that served as newspapers at the time, and started to follow Mercanton out of the room.

"Don't go," Roger said. He had to get used to it. It wouldn't help to be alone. "I want to know what's happened while I've been away." Marthe hesitated at the door, then closed it and came back into the room.

"Nothing happened," she said. "Except that Pensée is going to have puppies. She certainly has fooled us all." She hesitated a moment, then went on: "What is it? You're not just tired. Something has happened."

"Yes, something has happened." He wasn't going to cry.

He could feel the tears piling up behind his eyes. He must hold them back. Once they started to flow, they would never stop.

"Would it help to tell me about it? Or is it business?"

"No, it's not business." Roger stared ahead of him for a moment, knowing that he could hold himself in no longer, dreading what he must say.

"There was a girl. We were in love with each other. Last night, she killed herself." The memory of her came rushing back to him and he turned his face from Marthe, gasping at the harsh finality of his own words. A great broken sob was torn from him, and the tears came at last. He sat doubled over in the chair, uttering agonized irregular cries, wholly abandoned to his grief.

After awhile, he heard Marthe move and felt her hand on his shoulder, exerting a strong compassionate pressure. He fumbled for it blindly and held it in a tight grip. She fell to her knees in front of him and gathered him in her arms. He clung to her helplessly, his head buried in her breast, his whole body racked by spasms of despair. She held him strongly to her, stroking his hair. If only Jean Louis doesn't come in, she thought. If only he doesn't come. This means nothing. I can give him comfort. That is all. I hold him in my arms and comfort him. I can do that much. If only Jean Louis doesn't come.

Gradually his tears subsided. He was spent and ashamed for having so completely lost control. He lifted his head a little and tried to brush the tears away with his hands, taking deep breaths to steady himself. Marthe leaned away from him, keeping her hands on his shoulders.

"It's all right," he said. "I don't know what I'd have done if I couldn't have come here. It helps to be here."

"I'm glad you feel that," Marthe said gently. "It's what I would have wished."

CHAPTER

Nine

///

I

THE war was going to end soon. Roger knew it because
of the type of material passed on by his headquarters for
transmission. All through the first weeks of February, he
and Mercanton prepared messages dealing with the movements of whole divisions, the quantity of aircraft stationed
in various parts of France, and details of future Allied
strategy. It could only mean that the final push was under
way.

Roger struggled to keep his mind alert to these developments. But it was hard making himself believe it mattered.
He lived with the ghost of Danielle—Danielle laughing at
him, the two of them dreaming away the hours in front of
the fire, her swift beauty caught in his arms. If only she
had known. If only he had had more time. He lay in bed
at night, perfectly still, waiting for sleep to come, thinking
of her. He wished he could believe that she was near him
now, even in death, so that she would know . . . And then
the tears would come, soundlessly in the dark. As the days
passed, his tears gradually dried up, but the pain remained,
cutting into him, leaving him sore and raw. The guilt
grew in him, overpowering him, until he felt he must some-

how free himself of it. He had received several anxious letters from Carol, begging for news. He forced himself to answer with as much warmth as possible. It made him feel better, as if he were preserving something blameless in himself.

Actually, he thanked God for the work. Sometimes, he felt his mind go blank, and he would have to ask Mercanton to go over some problem again from the beginning. But it was the work that made life even remotely possible. There was so much to do. The near-disaster at Nice had to be straightened out. He was determined to maneuver Mercanton into such a strong position that he might have a fighting chance when brought to judgment. An obligation rested on him to assure justice, as he saw it, to the family. It was the only justification he could find for his betrayal of Danielle. After all, his guilt extended beyond Danielle. He had tangled this family in a grotesque lie. Unconsciously, he was prepared to offer himself as atonement, pitifully seeking absolution in their eyes and his own. But time was running out.

Shortly after the trip to Nice, he had found, while he was cleaning out his car, an identity card which had slipped down behind the seat. It was apparently one he had taken from M. Paul, which had somehow been separated from the others in the dark. He put it away, thinking to turn it in to his office on his next trip to Marseille. But later, thinking it over, he decided to keep it. He might find some use for it. He had no definite plans in mind, but you never could tell. . . .

The German reaction to Mercanton's renewed demands for money was encouraging. Yes, they were aware that

M. Paul had had to change his plans at the last minute. (Roger almost laughed at that touch.) Unfortunately, it seemed best to abandon the notion of passing money through go-betweens in Nice. If Mercanton would just hold on for a few more weeks, some satisfactory scheme would be worked out.

II

LATE in February an ambitious German project began to unfold on the radio. First they wanted to know how well Mercanton knew the mountains north of Nice. Not very well, Mercanton replied. It was an open front, they told him, rarely patrolled. They were in the habit of sending their men back and forth across the lines regularly in this area. Did Mercanton think he could get there without too much difficulty? Yes, Mercanton supposed he could. With these preliminaries out of the way, the Germans subsided for a few days.

Then, in the longest message Mercanton had yet received, they presented their plan. Blum wanted to see Mercanton. In addition to his pay there were large sums of money to be distributed to other agents in France. As their most trustworthy agent, Mercanton was the logical man to handle this matter. There were also important questions of future intelligence to be discussed—new objectives, changes in policy. It was felt that this could be accomplished best by a personal interview. In a small village a few kilometers east of St. Martin Vesubie there was a "safe house" frequently used in the passage of agents across the lines. The rendezvous would take place there. Mercanton would ask for the home of M. Peladeau. It was absolutely safe. A date for the meeting would be given as soon as Mercanton agreed to undertake the mission.

When he had decoded the message, Roger passed it over to Mercanton. It was the first time in weeks he had experienced a pleasurable excitement. "Well, what do you think of that?" he asked. Mercanton studied the message carefully.

"You would get much valuable information from such a meeting," he said. "Will you be able to get permission for me to do it?"

"I certainly think so. Of course, it might be a trap."

"I had thought of that." Mercanton read through the message once more. "It's hard to tell. They seem anxious for me to come."

"Yes. I hope they aren't too anxious. It might be dangerous, you know."

"I don't mind that. I hope I'll be able to prove my sincerity to your service. Perhaps if I do this job successfully, they'll be willing to forget the past."

"Of course. The more important your work, the better it is for you," Roger said, trying to feel the conviction he put into his voice.

"The only part of it I don't like is having to keep up the pretense with those people—Blum and whoever else comes. That will be difficult."

"You don't think you'll be able to fool them?"

"Oh, of course, I shall have to. But it won't be easy."

"Well, we'll have to tell them tomorrow morning that you'll do it. We can't wait for a decision from my headquarters. If they don't approve, we'll have to think of some excuse later."

<h1 style="text-align:center">III</h1>

ROGER delivered the message to his office and asked for immediate action on it. The next day, he was summoned by telephone to Marseille. It was the first time he had seen Meddling since the night in Nice. He found him cool and peremptory. His former joviality had been put aside.

"I got a very prompt response from Paris," he said. "They're very much interested in this Blum business. They want us to take the man as soon as possible."

"They want us to take the man?" Roger could scarcely believe his ears.

"Yes. They say they know who Blum is and they're very anxious to have him. They're sending a man down who's had a lot of experience with raiding parties to help you with the military end of it."

"But that's impossible. If we take Blum, Mercanton is finished. The Germans will know he's double-crossed them."

"That's right," said Meddling with malicious relish. "When you have Blum, you're to bring Mercanton in and turn him over to the French. Paris feels he's fulfilled his usefulness. The war'll be over soon. We can't play around with him forever."

"And then what?" Roger suddenly realized he was afraid. He had trouble getting his breath. He made a furious effort to control himself. Here it was at last.

"Why, then the French will give him a full-dress trial." Meddling was a little taken aback by Roger's apparent calm. "Our friend Mercanton is going to get his with all the trimmings."

"And what about the family?" Roger was surprised he was still able to speak.

"What about them? As far as I know, they're not mixed up in it. The French'll probably take all the old man's property and give the family their blessing."

"Do you have a copy of those orders from Paris?"

"Yes, as a matter of fact I have." Meddling handed a sheet of paper across his desk. He watched with a faint smile while Roger read it. He was a little disappointed. He had expected trouble. He knew this meant a lot to Roger in some incomprehensible way. He had thought he might explode, possibly even refuse the mission.

"This is the most idiotic idea I ever heard of," Roger burst out. He flung the paper back onto the desk and stood up angrily. He walked over to the window so that his back would be turned to Meddling. He didn't want his superior to see how much he was affected. He suspected Meddling of some part in the decision, but he knew there was nothing to do about it. The order came from Paris. He was beaten.

"What's the matter, Roger?" Meddling spoke with insinuating lightness. "You knew this would happen sometime. If you don't want to do the job, I can give it to someone else." Roger took a quick grip on himself and sat down again in front of Meddling. He replied casually:

"That's all right. I'll take care of it."

"I suppose you noticed you're to report to Paris when the job's finished. I'll be sorry to see you go."

"Thanks. By the way, did you find out what that guy in Nice was doing with all the identity cards?"

"Sure. He had no secrets from us. He picked them up from agents going back to the Fatherland. He thought you might want one. He brought them along to see which one fitted you best."

"Very thoughtful of him. Well, I guess that's everything. Let me know when the military expert arrives. We'll have a lot of planning to do."

IV

THAT night, Roger told Mercanton that the plan was to be carried out, but that Blum was to be taken. He didn't tell him of the sequel that was to follow. He could hardly expect Mercanton to carry out his difficult assignment with the knowledge that he was moving to his own death.

"But that will be dangerous, won't it?" Mercanton asked. "If Blum doesn't get back, the Germans will surely suspect me."

"Yes, there is that risk. But my headquarters feels sure that you can be protected. I can't tell you how. They wouldn't even tell me."

"Your service is very remarkable. I suppose it has ways of arranging such things." Mercanton seemed completely satisfied. He paused and then said thoughtfully: "You know, I would be much happier if your service considered me a full partner in this work. Do you think that if I carry out this job well, they will be convinced of my sincerity? It's not pleasant to trick a man into his own destruction. That's what I'll be doing with Blum."

"No, it's not pleasant," Roger said with an intensity that surprised Mercanton. "Sometimes we're forced into it. But don't worry about the future. You've done important work. It won't be forgotten." As he spoke, Roger knew that he had come to a decision. He wouldn't deliver Mercanton to the French. He felt a wonderful elation. This was what he had been waiting for. Here was the chance for redemption he had sought for weeks. His spirit soared with the knowledge that he had tricked this man for the last time. Now he would make good his promise. The identity card could be doctored to fit Mercanton. In some way Mercanton must, as Marthe had once suggested, simply disappear. It wouldn't be easy, but Roger felt sure he could manage it somehow.

The next few days were busy. The military expert arrived from Paris and Roger held several conferences with him. He turned out to be a quiet, serious, young lieutenant called Hollings. He and Roger decided to take a force of twelve men, all to be provided with civilian clothes, submachine guns and tear-gas grenades. They would have to wait until they could look over the lay of the land before they could plan their strategy.

Mercanton was more animated than Roger had ever seen him. He got out maps and located the village, and spent hours drawing up campaign plans. He thought of many small difficulties that Roger might otherwise have overlooked. As usual, Marthe had not been fully informed of the scheme, but she knew enough to watch the preparations with a mixture of amusement and concern.

One evening she said to Roger: "You know, you've made my husband very happy. He loves to be active. I don't know exactly what you're planning, but he acts as if he were going to capture the entire German Army single-handed. I hope you won't let him be a nuisance."

"No, indeed. He's being very helpful," Roger said sincerely.

"I'm glad of that. He's very much of a child, really. He loves to run things. This expedition will be good for him. He's been dying to get away from here for a little while."

"That's understandable," Roger said, wondering what Marthe would think of his plan for her husband's future.

"I want to ask you something," Marthe said, growing serious. "You probably won't want to tell me, but I'd like to know. Will your trip be dangerous?" She spoke calmly, but her tone demanded an honest answer. Roger hesitated, then looked her in the eye.

"Yes," he said. "It will be dangerous for your husband."

"Thank you," said Marthe quietly. "That's what I wanted to know."

V

IN THE first week of March, the Germans sent their final instructions. The meeting was to take place in one week at nine o'clock in the evening at the house of M. Peladeau, as already designated. Mercanton was advised to wear old clothes so as not to be conspicuous. He would probably have to make the few kilometers from St. Martin to the village by foot. There would be friends at the meeting whom Mercanton would doubtless be glad to see.

Discussing the message, Roger said to Mercanton: "You know, I think it would be better if you used a false identity card. No point using your own name when you don't have to. I've got one for you, but we'll have to change photographs." So, together, they painstakingly mounted a picture of Mercanton on the new card and he became, for the time being, Michel Dussault, of Nîmes.

They left the farm on Sunday, two days before the scheduled meeting. Mercanton wore his oldest clothes, but carried with him a splendid array of equipment—maps and flashlights, a compass and a pair of field glasses. He was in high spirits. Roger tried to match his mood. He wouldn't allow himself to think that this might be the last time he would see the family. Perhaps the last time Mercanton would see them, too.

They all gathered round to watch the departure. The younger children were pleased with all the excitement, hanging on the car with wide-eyed interest. Dominique stood apart sullenly, having said a perfunctory farewell to his father. Marthe put on a fine performance, laughing and teasing her husband about his elaborate preparations, until the last minute when she suddenly clung to him and murmured: "Take care. Take care, dear one." Mercanton extricated himself as quickly as possible. Roger saw the tears gathering in Marthe's eyes. He hurriedly busied himself with the car. He felt his throat tighten. He didn't try to speak. He simply waved and let the car roll down the drive.

"Well, we're on our way," said Mercanton. "I think I have everything." Roger kept his eyes on the road and nodded.

They reached St. Martin late that afternoon. Roger had arranged to meet Hollings and his task force at the American Command Post that evening. He and Mercanton were to keep away from the Americans as much as possible. They took rooms separately at a small hotel and settled down to wait. After dinner, Roger met Hollings and it was decided that the next day Roger would make a reconnaissance of the nearby village, with special attention to the Peladeau house. They had learned its location from the local gendarmerie. Roger went back to the hotel and looked in on Mercanton before he went to bed. He was reading, stretched out on the bed in his cold shabby room.

"This isn't much like La Violette," he said wistfully. "I haven't been away from home for a long time. It seems very strange."

"This isn't much of a place for an outing."

"No. I'll be glad to get home again. I've been thinking. I hope Blum won't want to know much about where I've been getting all the information I've been sending."

"Thank God, we've been vague about your sources. You can mention one or two people and say you'd rather not reveal any more. They can't very well insist."

"What if it turns out to be a trap, after all?"

"I'm going to look the place over tomorrow. We'll figure something out afterwards. I'm going to get some sleep. Are you all right?"

"Yes, indeed. But I'm glad we don't have to stay here long. Do you think we'll get home on Wednesday?"

"Sure. We might even leave Tuesday night. We'll see how things work out." Roger went thoughtfully to his own room and went to bed. Yes, they would wait and see how things worked out.

VI

ROGER started off on foot early the next morning. He instructed Mercanton to stay close to the hotel until he returned. It turned out to be a tiring walk. The road was mountainous and the snow was still heavy on the ground. There were numerous road blocks but civilians with proper credentials were allowed to pass. When he reached the village, he found it even smaller than he had expected—a single twisting street not more than a few hundred yards long, closely packed with shuttered, bare-faced houses. He found the Peladeau house by following instructions, a house just like its neighbors, with the door opening directly onto the street. He walked past it, giving it only a casual glance. He tried to circle around the little town, but found that on one side the hill fell away sharply just behind the row of houses. On the other side, Roger found a path that must have led past the Peladeau house, though he couldn't recognize it from the back, up through some steep fields and into a wood. There were so few people about that Roger made his survey as rapidly as possible. He was too conspicuous. He was soon back on the road to St. Martin. When he was out of sight of the village, he stopped long enough to make a rough sketch of the street and the surrounding country, including as many details as he was able to remember. Back in St. Martin, Roger went directly to see Hollings.

"This isn't going to be easy," he told the young lieutenant, showing him the sketch he'd made. "We could surround the house and pick them off when they come out, but we've got to take them alive. We might be able to do it with gas. There're only two ways for them to get to the house—the front door on the street or by the back way along this path. We don't want to prevent them going to the house, but I would like to know how many of them there are. The trouble is, it's so damn hard to set up a watch. It's a deserted village. Anybody hanging around would stick out like a sore thumb."

Roger went on to point out other difficulties. If the Germans were taking anything like the same precautions the Americans were, it was impossible to send Hollings and his group into the village en masse. They would be instantly spotted. It was decided to send the men off the following afternoon in groups of twos and threes, to gather behind a rock formation Roger had noticed near the road just outside of the village. There was also the problem of their arms. Civilians carrying sub-machine guns would undoubtedly arouse comment Hollings promised to see that all arms were disguised in parcels or carried in suitcases. One man would be sent into the village early the next morning. He wouldn't be able to do a thorough job of surveillance, but by moving about he would be able to keep a partial check on the house during the day. As soon as it was dark, two men would be stationed at either end of the short main street, and two men would take up positions just off the path where it passed closest to the backs of the houses. At nine-fifteen, any traffic in and out of the village was to be stopped and carefully checked. By that time, Mercanton would be having his interview. Each station was to be provided with a whistle to be used to summon help in case of emergency. The remainder of the party would take positions in doorways near Roger in

front of the Peladeau house. Roger hoped that Mercanton
would be able to complete his business quickly and report
to him on the situation inside the house: how many men
were in the German party and when they planned to leave.
The best Roger hoped for was that they could all be taken
quietly as they left the house by the front door. Roger
couldn't wait for daylight without revealing his presence.
If the Germans weren't planning to leave that night, it
would be necessary to go in and get them. Roger hoped
that Mercanton would have obtained all the money and
significant papers, so that if there were a few casualties no
great harm would be done.

When all details had been settled with Hollings, Roger
returned to his hotel to join Mercanton. He found him
sitting forlornly in his room studying his maps.

"You know," he said. "I've found that all the mileages
on these maps are incorrect. For instance, it says here that
it's twenty-seven kilometers between Cannes and Nice. I
particularly noticed yesterday on your meter that it's only
twenty-two kilometers."

"Maybe they've shortened the roads since the maps were
made."

"That's possible. I hadn't thought of that." Mercanton
bent over the maps once more.

"I've been doing a little map making, myself," Roger
said. "Let's get this business straight between us and then
we can forget about it until tomorrow night. Here's the
set-up. As soon as you go in at nine o'clock we'll have
the house surrounded. I hope you can get the money and
the names and addresses quickly and come right out."

"I will be anxious to come out quickly, too. I hope they

don't ask me too much about the work I've been doing. I'm not very good at lying."

"I don't think you'll have to lie. You can say you have good connections with the Americans. In fact, I think you ought to boast about it a little. They may wonder how you get the Americans to talk so much, but you can be secretive about that. Say it's one of the secrets of your trade."

"That's true enough." Mercanton chuckled unexpectedly. "I've often wondered where the information comes from, myself. Marthe ought to be doing this job. She'd enjoy it."

"She'd be good at it," Roger laughed too. "She'd have everybody talking about their wives and babies and they'd forget what they came for. Well, anyway, while you're in there, I want you to try to find out how many of them there are and when they're planning to go back to their own side. I've been thinking what you ought to do if they're pulling any tricks on us. I think you'd better just play along with them. They won't want to do you any harm. If anything, they'll want to take you with them. There are only two ways to leave the place, front and back. If they want to keep you with them, you'll just have to go along until our men show up and then fall on the ground and stay out of the line of fire until things are under control."

"I hope that won't happen. In the dark, the line of fire is apt to be almost anywhere."

"I don't think it'll happen. Well, I guess that's everything. If, by any chance, they're planning to stay over night and want to keep you with them, we'll just have to come in and get them. If we wait 'til daylight they'll see us and have a chance to destroy their papers."

"They'll have a chance to destroy me, too."

"Yes, that's true. Well, I'll wait 'til two o'clock and then if you haven't come out, we'll use gas. That won't be very pleasant for you, but it won't do you any permanent damage."

"I see it's going to be a very entertaining evening," Mercanton said drily. "Will I be armed?"

"I've wondered about that. I don't see what good it would do. But if it would make you feel more comfortable, I can give you a gun. I suppose that would be better. I'll get one for you later."

Roger and Mercanton spent the rest of the day sitting restlessly in the latter's room. They didn't want to be seen together on the streets. Occasionally they spoke of ships or planes, and then Mercanton would talk for long stretches, completely absorbed in his subject, while Roger thought of other things. He was impatient to get the rendezvous with Blum out of the way. He was more concerned with what was to follow. That was to be his vindication. Already, he felt as if his burden of guilt had been lifted. But, somehow he dreaded the moment. That he should help Mercanton evade his judgment had assumed a kind of melodramatic unreality during these quiet, expectant hours they had spent together. He never doubted that he would carry it through, but the thought of proposing it to Mercanton embarrassed him slightly. Mercanton was so clearly not made for intrigue. His participation in this plot to capture a German spy-master had about it a kind of gallant incongruity. He was doing his best to fit himself into a set of circumstances that had no meaning for him. He was successful to the extent that he thought of it in terms of maps (with incorrect mileages) and ingenious stratagems and mechanical devices—flashlights and compasses and tear-gas bombs. The fact that there might be larger implications, connected with a great conflict of ideologies, was lost on him. How could Roger tell such a man he would be shot, having served his purpose? How could he suggest he choose instead a life of anonymity and flight? Yet he must do it or abandon him and his family to their ruin. Roger did not think of the consequences to himself. He could probably get away with it. He would simply report that Mercanton had vanished. There would be a search for him. But nobody knew about the false identity card. Nobody would be looking for Michel Dussault. . . .

Somehow the day passed and it was finally time to go to bed. "A big day tomorrow," Roger said to Mercanton. "I'm going to get some sleep."

"I don't sleep very well in strange places," Mercanton said fretfully. "I didn't sleep at all last night. I hope Marthe doesn't have any trouble with the furnace. I showed Dominique how to take care of it."

"They'll probably get along all right. Marthe knows how to manage things."

"Yes, but she's not used to being alone. Do you think we might go back tomorrow night?"

"Sure, if it's not too late," Roger said shortly. "It's a pretty long drive."

"Well, good night."

"Good night. I hope you get some sleep."

VII

Roger rejoined Hollings at the American Command Post the next day, checking arrangements, and giving final briefing to the dozen men. As the afternoon wore on, Roger dispatched them in twos and threes, laden with large bundles of arms and ammunition and looking a little shamefaced in their ill-fitting civilian clothes. He was to join them at seven o'clock at the rock ledge. The man who had been sent into the village that morning was to report at the same place at the same time. When the last men had left and Hollings too had started on his way, Roger returned to the hotel. Mercanton was waiting for him, ready to leave.

"I brought you a gun," Roger said, and showed him how to strap the holster under his arm. "You'll be able to pick up something to eat when you get there. There's a café. You'll have plenty of time. Be sure to be at the Peladeau house promptly at nine. When you come out, just walk up the street until you're out of sight of the house. Then wait for me, I'll be watching for you. Now, have you got everything straight?"

"Yes. I'll be very agreeable with Blum, and leave him as quickly as possible."

"Good. And be sure you find out when they're planning to start back to the other side. If you should run into any sort of trouble before you get to the house, just yell. The place is going to be crawling with us. One of us will hear you."

"I don't think there will be any trouble."

"I hope not. Good luck." He and Mercanton shook

hands. "I'm going to give you a head start. I'll be only a few minutes behind you."

Roger reached the rendezvous point behind the rocks at a few minutes before seven. Everybody was there except the advance scout. It was already dark, with just a faint afterglow of day in the sky. It was clear and cold and the men were shifting about restlessly, stamping their feet on the ground. They spoke in low murmurs. They had unwrapped and assembled their guns and their pockets were bulging with ammunition and grenades. One or two of them were puffing on cigarettes. Roger reminded them that there was to be no more smoking when they moved into the village. At a few minutes past seven, the last member of the party slipped in silently behind the rocks.

"I'm glad you got here," Roger said to him. "Anything doing in town?"

"Absolutely nothing, sir. It's as dead as a doornail. Just a few people moving around during the day."

"Did you see anybody entering the house?"

"Not a soul, sir. One old guy came out this morning."

"You think people might have gone in without your seeing them?"

"Sure, sir. I couldn't watch it all the time. But I don't think there could've been many."

"OK. Fine. Listen, all of you. Gather round." Roger spoke softly, looking into the dim outlines of the faces surrounding him. "You all know what to do. The six of you that are going to take the road and the path, just stand by until nine-fifteen and then don't let anybody past. You've got your whistles in case anything turns up. OK. You can take off. Wait a second. Check your watches.

It's seven-fourteen. OK. And keep your guns out of sight as much as possible." Roger waited while six figures moved out of sight. He turned back to the ones that were left. "All right. The rest of you are going to stay with me. I'm going to station you in doorways along the street. Just stay put until you get the word from Lieutenant Hollings or me. If we meet anybody in the streets, just act natural. Don't do anything that'll look funny. We're going to have a long wait. If you want to move around a little, that's OK, but don't talk to each other. Let's go."

Roger led the straggling group back to the road. Just before they entered the town, he indicated to Hollings the path that led off across the fields. A little farther on, two of the men were lounging against a fence adjoining the first house of the village. Roger and his party passed without exchanging any sign of recognition. The little street was dark. Here and there lights showed between the cracks of doors and shutters, but for the most part the village seemed already asleep. As he approached the Peladeau house from the opposite side of the street, Roger distributed his men with a gesture of his hand in doorways and recesses in the buildings. When all the men had been assigned places, he and Hollings walked on a little farther.

"You better go check the other boys and see they're all placed properly," Roger whispered when they were a safe distance from the house. "Did you notice that place that looked like a garage we passed a minute ago? I'm going back there. You come join me." He turned back while Hollings continued on up the street. So far, they had encountered no townspeople. Passing several of the men in their doorways, Roger noted with satisfaction that they were well hidden in shadow.

The garage he had selected for his own position was almost directly opposite the Peladeau house. The doors were deeply recessed so he could stand well back from the street and observe all arrivals and departures across the way. He could see a light burning behind one of the shutters of the house. He looked at his watch. It was not yet eight. It was going to be a grim wait. Roger had dressed himself warmly, but already the cold was beginning to creep in at unprotected places. He tried swinging his arms gently, but found that he was warmer when he stayed still, huddled inside his clothes. In a little while, Hollings joined him.

"Everything's OK," he said, little puffs of steam escaping from his mouth as he spoke. "Nobody's seen anything. I moved the boys a little farther up the path to be sure nobody can slip behind them. Visibility's pretty good back there. They'll see it if anybody starts moving around."

"What about them? Will they be seen?"

"No, I've got them near some trees. Anything else to do?"

"No. Just wait. I'll be glad when this is over."

"Me too. The boys are going to freeze to death."

VIII

THEY stood against the wall, close together for added warmth. Roger tried to think of something agreeable to make the time pass quickly. But it was no use. His mind produced only half-images, fragments of thoughts, jarred out of focus by every sound in the night. Once, two men passed, indistinctly cursing the war and the weather. Somewhere, a bell was striking the hours and half-hours— a thin sharp note that seemed to intensify the cold. Time had slowed to an endless minute. Roger tried not to look at his watch. After awhile, he sent Hollings out to make another round of the men. He came back with nothing to report. They resumed their position against the wall.

Roger tried counting to relieve the monotony. When he got into the big numbers he found it entertaining trying to keep all the figures in their proper order. He was saying to himself: "Three thousand, five hundred and forty-nine," when the bell started to strike nine o'clock. He heard foot-steps coming down the street and then recognized Mercanton's outline as he stopped in front of the Peladeau house. He watched as the door opened and Mercanton disappeared inside.

"That was your guy?"

"Yeah. I hope to God he gets it over with quickly." Roger moved out slightly, preparing to follow Mercanton as soon as he reappeared. Half an hour ought to be enough for the meeting. It might even be over in fifteen minutes. He pulled out his .45 to make sure it was cocked. He whispered over his shoulder to Hollings: "All set, in case anybody comes out with him?" and he heard Hollings mutter an affirmative. He held himself taut, ready to move fast. By nine-thirty, he felt his muscles beginning to ache with the strain. As the hands of his watch moved on towards ten he began to wonder angrily what was going on in the house. A few minutes past ten, he felt Hollings move up beside him.

"You think he'll be out soon?" he asked.

"Dammit, he ought to be out now," Roger murmured impatiently. They stood side by side, straining for something to happen. Everything was quiet across the way. The light still shone dimly behind the shutter. By ten-thirty, he had begun to suspect the worst. So it was a trap, after all. Or perhaps Mercanton had made some slip. He hoped he hadn't given the whole game away. Looking at his watch again he saw it was almost eleven.

"Listen," he whispered to Hollings. "Go out and tell the men next to us to be ready to follow me if more than one person comes out of that building. Then you'd better go check the others."

"You think something has gone wrong?"

"I don't know. Get back here as quickly as you can." Hollings hurried out and Roger could hear his footsteps moving lightly in the street, pausing momentarily as he spoke to the men in the nearby doorways. It was almost eleven-thirty when he returned.

"What in hell took you so long?" Roger whispered sharply.

"One of the boys has jammed his gun. I tried to fix it."

"Is it all right now?"

"No, I couldn't do anything with it. Anything doing here?"

"Not a damn thing."

"What are you going to do?"

"I told my man I'd wait 'til two o'clock. Then we'll have to go in. The light's still on. I guess that means they might still be talking."

Ten minutes later, the light suddenly blinked off. The house across the street was in darkness. Roger felt his breath coming fast. It was true then. The Germans were on to Mercanton.

"Get ready," Roger said. "They may be coming out." But as they watched, a light glowed in an upstairs window. Whatever had happened, the household was apparently going to bed. Roger turned to Hollings and was about to speak when there was a sharp burst of fire from the end of town.

"What the hell!" he exclaimed.

"Damn fools," Hollings growled.

"Get down there and find out what's going on. I'll take care of things here." Roger's nerves were tightening. His tidy planning seemed to be going to pieces. There were so many things that might go wrong. Could there be another exit that they had overlooked? Over the roofs, maybe, or. . . . But it was too late to think about that. They had made their plan. Now they had to stick to it. He hoped nobody had pulled any rough stuff on Mercanton. Then he remembered what he had in store for the Frenchman. Six of one. . . . It would be simpler really if something did happen to him. Well, the evening wasn't over yet, he thought grimly. In a few minutes, Hollings ducked back into the shelter of the doorway.

"Sorry, Chandler," he said. "It was that gun. It came unjammed."

"I hope you threw it away. Anything doing down there?"

"Not a thing. The boys are getting pretty cold."

"We'll have some excitement for them before we're through."

"What are you going to do now?"

"Nothing. Wait some more. Something may've happened we didn't count on. We've got to hold off until two." The house across the street was dark and silent. Nothing stirred in the whole village. The cold tones of the bell sounded the half-hour and then the single note of one o'clock. Every muscle in Roger's body was aching with the wait. He tried shifting his position but could find no relief. He felt he had to do something or remain paralyzed there forever.

"Goddammit," he muttered to the hunched figure at his side. "I'm going to hold on fifteen more minutes and then I'm going to fill that house with gas."

"That's all right with me," Hollings said. "I hope they try to get tough. I'd like to kill a few Germans for tonight's work."

"OK. Tell the men to get ready. I'm going over and try to open a window. Keep me covered. When I give the signal, you can start throwing, upstairs and down."

Roger left Hollings and walked up the street a little way. He crossed over and doubled back, keeping close to the wall. When he reached the house, he put his hand on the door knob and turned it slowly. He leaned slightly against the door. It was locked and solid in its frame. He went to the window which had shown a light all evening. The blind was loose and Roger was able to work his hand behind it and undo the catch. He swung the blind back and held his breath when it made a long squeak that seemed to echo in the silent street. He dropped quickly to the ground, all other senses suspended in listening. He heard no sound come from within the building. The blind protected a casement window. Roger slipped his knife between the frame and felt it hold against the latch. He pushed upwards and the latch gave way. The window swung open slightly. He pushed against it and looked into the room, ready to drop at the first sign of danger. He could see the faint outlines of furniture and smell the heavy odor of tobacco smoke come out to meet the sharp night air. He turned and hurried back across the street. Hollings had the six men bunched together in the shadow of the garage.

"Hold the grenades," Roger said. "This is too easy. We'll just walk in on them. Keep your guns ready. And for God's sake be quiet. Come on." Roger led the men back by his roundabout way to the open window. He lifted himself over the sill and waited just inside for the others to follow him. As each man pulled himself into the room, Roger directed him with a nudge and a whisper into a dark corner. He could hear the faint pop of his lips as they shaped a command. To the last man, he whispered: "OK. Close the blind." He crept over to the door and felt along the wall for the light switch. His hand fumbled, and then found it. He turned on the light and swung around, his gun in his hand.

He and his men faced each other across an empty room. Several chairs were pulled close to the fireplace where some coals still glowed, and there was a bottle and some empty glasses on a table. Roger beckoned to the men. He crossed the hall and turned on the lights in the room beyond. It was a dining room, also empty.

"A couple of you look in there." Roger shaped the words with his mouth and pointed to an open door leading into the back of the house. They returned in a moment. "Nothing in there," they signalled.

"OK. Up we go." Roger led the way on tiptoe up the stairs and the others followed in single file. When he reached the landing, he paused and heard heavy breathing coming from behind a closed door. Roger went quickly to the door and then gestured once more to his companions. They spilled quickly into the other rooms and immediately rejoined him, shaking their heads. Roger turned and opened the door and switched on the light. An old man lay on a bed against the wall, snoring gently. Roger crossed over to him and prodded him sharply with his gun. The old man leaped up with a cry.

"Be quiet," Roger said in a menacing undertone. "Where are the others?"

"They've gone." The old man spoke French with a thick Italian accent. His eyes were blank with sleep and confusion. Roger turned to Hollings.

"Look in the attic," he said. Hollings left the room with two of the men. Roger could hear them moving around above. He turned back to the old man who was sitting in the midst of the rumpled bed-clothes, a woolen undershirt covering his slight body.

"Where did they go?" Roger demanded.

"Who? I don't understand," said the old man, blinking his eyes and assuming now a look of elaborate innocence.

"The people you were just talking about. That's who." Hollings came back into the room as Roger spoke.

"There's nothing upstairs," he reported.

"Have one of the men take care of this old fool," Roger ordered. "I can't be bothered to beat anything out of him now. Let's go downstairs. I want to see if there's a cellar in the house. They may be down there." The raiding party rushed down the stairs and back to the kitchen, where Roger found a door leading down to the cellar.

"Be careful," he cautioned as they started down. There was no light. When he reached the foot of the stairs, Roger switched on his flashlight, swinging it in a rapid arc before him. There was no one there. It was less a cellar than the foundations of the house. The floor was of hard packed earth. Roger swung the light around the walls. There was a pile of wood in one corner. Otherwise, the place was bare. He lowered his light and saw a broad wooden door set into the floor near the opposite wall.

"Wait a minute," he exclaimed. He crossed quickly over and pulled back the door. Directing his flashlight downwards, he could see steps leading into the ground. So that was it. Nobody had been seen entering the building all day. Christ, he'd been a fool. Hollings was at his side.

"What is it?" he asked.

"We're going to find out. Come on." Roger raced down the stairs, and up a passageway. Empty racks for wine were banked along both walls. A little way along, there was a sharp turn. The racks ended and the passage narrowed into a rough tunnel cut out of the earth. Roger slowed down. The men were at his heels. They advanced cautiously for several minutes until they came to a blank wall with stairs mounting to a trap-door overhead. Roger gestured for silence and ascended carefully. He pushed back the trap-door and sprang out with one movement, his gun in his hand. He found himself in a small thicket of shrubbery. He looked around him. Down across the fields he could see the shape of the village. Close behind him the wood began. Hollings and his men came crowding out of the small opening in the ground.

"Well, that finishes us for the night," Roger said. He was seized with a sort of panic. His mission had failed. The Germans were gone, Mercanton with them. Maybe— the thought struck him a numbing blow—maybe Mercanton had doubled-crossed the Americans, too. He heard Hollings ask:

"What are we going to do now?"

"What can we do?" Roger said disgustedly. "Go to bed, I guess."

"Christ, oughtn't we to follow them?" They continued to whisper, out of habit.

"How can we follow them? They've got two hours start on us. They probably cleared out when that old bastard went to bed."

"We can try. They may have stopped somewhere farther along. This is important, isn't it?"

"Sure it's important. But what do you want to do? Follow their footsteps in the snow? An hour's walk in that direction will probably take you right to a German installation." Roger felt an unreasonable anger rising in him.

"That'd be fine. I'm just in the mood to take care of some Heinies after sitting in that street for six whole hours. I'm going to get the men together." Hollings took out his whistle and blew several long blasts.

"You can play Boy Scout if . . ." Roger began heatedly, but left off in the middle of a word. From not far off, a voice had called "Dulin." Roger recognized it instantly as Mercanton's.

"Jean Louis," he shouted, and the voice called back from the wood: "Up here."

"Hallelujah," Roger cried, and he and his men raced up the slope. Just within the fringe of the wood, they found Mercanton sitting on a fallen tree, his revolver held in front of him. Two men were standing about five feet away.

"Look out," he called as the Americans approached. "Don't get in front of me."

"Are there any others?" Roger asked. Mercanton shook his head. "OK, let's have some light." Several flashlights cut through the dark, focusing on the two men. Roger saw a tall, sour-looking middle-aged man and beside him, a short, stooped man with a huge head whose slight body seemed swallowed up in a worn great-coat. They looked blank and sheepish, averting their heads and blinking in the sudden glare. The smaller man recovered himself and looked up, smiling winningly.

"Who is in charge . . . ?" he began in a silky whisper.

"You can save the talk for later. You'll have plenty of time." Roger turned to his men.

"Well, there they are. Let's take care of them." Several of the Americans moved in beside them, covering them with their guns. Hollings stepped into the light and went through their pockets. Each had a revolver. He hand-cuffed the men to each other. When he was finished, Roger said: "Let's get going." Hollings and the five soldiers fell in behind the prisoners and started down the hill towards the village. Four of the men who had been stationed below, hurrying up from the other direction, joined them. Roger turned back to Mercanton.

"You ought to get a medal for this," he said happily. "Did you get the money?" Mercanton slumped on the log, smiling wanly.

"Yes, I have the money, and lists of names and everything. I'm tired. I was afraid you weren't going to get here."

"Come on," Roger said. "Let's go." He helped Mercanton to his feet. "Who are they?"

"The tall one is Charlot. You remember my mentioning him. He was my friend. The other—the one who calls himself Blum—that's the one I saw in Paris. You know. I told you about him. I think he's very important."

Of course. Hilburger. A good night's work, Roger thought to himself. "There weren't any others?" he asked.

"Yes. There is a man at the house. I suppose he's Peladeau."

"We've taken care of him. But how did you get up here? What happened?" They were walking slowly towards the village.

"I was following your instructions." Mercanton's voice was flat and expressionless. "They had a great deal to talk about. Nothing important, but I couldn't think of any excuse to leave before they were finished. It was very unpleasant, having to laugh and joke with them. I wanted to get it over with as soon as possible."

"I can understand that," Roger said sympathetically.

"I wonder if you can. I felt almost . . . unclean. It wasn't nice. I think I did it rather well, too. That made it worse, somehow. Well, when they were ready to leave, they insisted on showing me their secret passage. I thought it would look suspicious if I refused. I suppose you've seen it?"

"Yes, we found it. But why didn't you hold them then?"

"It would have been difficult. There were three of them. Besides, you told me to go with them. I thought we'd be stopped by your men when we were outside. When we came out in the field I started to walk a little way with them and then we heard firing down below. That seemed to make them nervous and they started to hurry away. Your men were nowhere about, so I thought I'd better not let them leave."

"Thank God for that. They didn't give you any trouble?"

"I'm glad you're pleased. No, they saw I would shoot them if they moved. I would rather have shot them than sit facing them for two hours. At first, they seemed to think I was out of my mind. Then they offered me money. Finally, they tried to frighten me. They told me that their men would come to find them in a little while. I didn't see what I could do about it. I just hoped you would get there first."

"Why didn't you come right down with them?"

"It was too dangerous in the dark. I didn't know what had happened in the village. I knew you were going into the house at two o'clock. I hoped you would find me. Otherwise, I was going to wait until daylight." They had reached the juncture of the path and the road. Hollings and the men were waiting.

"You'd better go pick up the other character at the house," Roger said. "I suppose the two boys are still waiting at the other end of town. You'll have to call them in, too." They waited until the whole group was assembled and then they began the dreary walk back to St. Martin.

When they reached St. Martin and the prisoners had been dispatched to the American Command Post for safe-keeping, Mercanton seemed to revive. He tried to hold Roger in his room, plying him with questions about the evening and filling in the details of his own adventure. But Roger was tired, and he dreaded the job he would have to face the next day. He excused himself and went to bed.

IX

THE next morning, Hollings stopped by the hotel. The prisoners had been loaded into one of his trucks and his men were ready to take off.

"You go ahead," Roger said. "I'll be along a little later. You'll report to Major Meddling in Marseille. I'll be there some time this afternoon." Roger returned to Mercanton and they had breakfast together. The Frenchman looked rested and was eager to get started.

"It will be good to get home," he said, bright with antici-pation. "Marthe won't believe all we've been through. You'll have to tell her or she'll never believe it. If we hurry we'll get there before the children are home from school." He was so busy with their departure that he seemed unaware of Roger's lack of response. Once on the road, he occupied himself with his maps, checking the mile-age and exclaiming whenever he found an incorrect nota-tion. At last, he put them aside and said: "Have you been told what we're to say to the Germans now?"

"We have to talk about that," Roger said. He drove on

a little farther and turned off the main road onto a narrow
lane. There was a house in the distance but no one was in
sight.

"What are you doing?" Mercanton demanded. "This
isn't the right road." Roger pulled the car over to the side
of the lane and stopped.

"There are things I have to talk to you about," Roger
said with an effort. How could he possibly begin?

"Oh, very well," said Mercanton, subdued by Roger's
tone.

"You see, you're not going home. You're not going to
carry on your work with the Germans. That is . . ."

"But I don't understand . . ." Mercanton began as Roger
paused.

"Wait a minute, please," Roger cried out desperately.
"I have orders to deliver you to the French authorities in
Marseille. You're to be tried for treason."

"But that's impossible," Mercanton gasped. "When?
Have I done something wrong?"

"No. That is, you've done fine work since you've been
with us."

"Well, then, what is this all about?" Mercanton asked,
momentarily reassured.

"Good God, think a minute. You were captured as an
enemy agent. You're to be tried and punished."

"But I've been working with you. You said yourself . . ."

"Forget everything I've said," Roger exclaimed violently.
"I've been lying to you."

"You've been lying?" Mercanton's voice was mild with
disbelief.

"Yes, I've been lying. The whole damn thing has been lies all along. I had to. How else could I work with you?"

"You mean, you've known all along that . . . that it would end like this?"

"Yes. At least, I've been pretty sure. Now I have the orders."

"But that's monstrous. How could you do such a thing?" Mercanton seemed to struggle for comprehension.

"Of course, it's monstrous. Don't think I've wanted it like this. That's just it—" Roger paused and went on eagerly. "I'm going to help you escape."

"You're going to do what?"

"I'm going to help you get away. You've got your false identity card. I want you to leave me now and disappear."

"That's impossible."

"Why is it impossible? I'll report that you disappeared from the hotel. Nobody knows about the identity card. They'll never look for Michel Dussault."

"But you have your orders."

"Yes, I have my orders. They're part of the whole dirty mess."

"You must carry them out."

"I'm not going to carry them out," Roger declared with blazing determination. "They're wrong and you know it. You've got to get away." Mercanton was silent for a moment.

"I'd be caught," he said at last, with finality.

"Why should you be caught? You'll have a good chance. And even if you are . . ." Roger hesitated. He had started to say, "What difference will it make?" but the words sounded brutally indifferent.

"That's just it. If I'm caught, they'll be much harder on me."

"Christ, don't you understand? They can't be harder on you. They're going to take all your property away. You'll sit in jail for awhile and then you'll be shot."

"No, no, that's too much," Mercanton said with exasperation. "I don't believe you. They couldn't do it. You said yourself that the things I've done would count in my favor."

"Please listen to me." Roger was pleading. "I've told you I was lying. I'm telling you the truth now."

"You're being very kind, but I'm sure you must be mistaken. What about last night? Those men would have escaped if it hadn't been for me."

"I know that. But do you think that will make any difference? You were an enemy spy. That's all they care about."

"I can't understand." Mercanton shook his head. Self-pity was beginning to blur his voice. "If I run away, they'll surely seize my property, anyway. It's all in my name. Marthe won't be able to stop them. What will become of my family?"

"That's just it. If you go back now, there'll be a public trial. Your children will know all about it."

"It can't happen like that," Mercanton cried, agonized protest in his voice. "It would be better if I were dead. You should have arranged it so that something happened to me last night."

"But don't you understand? I'm giving you a chance to get away. They can't try a man they haven't got."

"They can announce in the papers that they're looking

for me. Besides, I'm not a criminal. I wouldn't know what to do. I'd be caught. No, you must take me to Marseille, or wherever you're supposed to take me. I'll hope for the best."

"You've got to understand there is no best," Roger was pleading once more. He was beginning to wonder himself what solution there could be. Mercanton probably *would* be caught. And yet there was the family. There was little to do for Mercanton. But he must save the family. He went on uncertainly: "There's nothing else to do. You must try to get away."

"There could have been another way." Mercanton spoke in tragic tones.

"What do you mean?"

"I tell you, it would be better if I were dead," Mercanton cried with sudden passion. "You should have told me. They couldn't take anything from Marthe. I'd have killed myself if you had told me."

"We needed you. That's why I couldn't tell you," Roger said harshly. And suddenly . . . he knew what he must do. He wondered for an instant why he hadn't known it all along. He felt himself go cold inside. "Get out of the car," he said abruptly.

"But just a minute." Mercanton turned to him in alarm.

"We can't talk all day. Get out of the car."

"But we have to arrange things . . ."

"Get out of the car," Roger almost shouted. He opened his door and got out. Mercanton followed suit hastily.

"I want to know how I should . . ." he began nervously.

"Go on. Start walking," Roger commanded. There was

a compelling warning in his voice. Mercanton took a few
steps and turned back.

"It's just that . . ."

"Keep walking. Don't turn back," Roger screamed, losing control of his voice. Mercanton turned and hurried
on. Roger's hand slipped inside his coat and he pulled out
his .45. A scene from their Christmas together flashed
through his mind—the pellets from the toy cannon bouncing off Mercanton's head. "You'd better surrender,"
Marthe had said. "Roger is a dangerous man." He lifted
the gun. His hand was trembling. He steadied it, took
careful aim and fired. Mercanton paused in the middle of a
step and then, with a wrenching convulsion, he seemed to
fling himself to the ground.

X

ROGER remembered little of the next few hours. He acted
automatically, his mind in a state of protective suspension.
He delivered Mercanton's body to the Military Police at
Nice, after first going through his pockets and removing
the false identity card. Somehow, he covered the road between Nice and Marseille. When he reached his headquarters, he went directly to a small room upstairs where he
was in the habit of writing his reports. It took only a
single sheet of paper to record the final episode in the Mercanton case.

At the end of the report, he wrote: "When I told him
he was to be turned over to the French, Mercanton seemed
to lose control of himself. He asked me to stop the car, and
when I did so he got out. I thought he just wanted to

relieve himself, but suddenly he began to run. I ordered him to halt but he turned off toward a field on the side of the road. I was forced to fire on him. The body has been given into the custody of the Military Police at Nice."

Roger carried the report downstairs to Meddling's office.

CHAPTER
Ten

‹‹‹

I

EVERYTHING was working out perfectly. Meddling had accepted his report without question. Roger wandered around Marseille, waiting for night to come. Meddling had agreed that he should be the one to tell Marthe, but he didn't want to reach the farm until the family had finished dinner. That way, he could talk to Marthe quietly without upsetting the household routine.

His mind was working slowly, dimmed by a nerveless lassitude. He was so conditioned to juggling fact and fiction that already this morning's events had lost their sharp outline. It would be hard telling Marthe. He must get Mercanton to help him. No, no, no. That was just it. Mercanton was dead, shot while trying to escape. No, that wouldn't do, either. Mercanton had been shot accidentally, gallantly fulfilling his duty. There. Keep it straight. Think about it a little while and it became true. Add some details, in case there were questions. What was wrong with that? People didn't want the truth. Leave them their illusions. And where did the whole truth lie, anyway? Mercanton was dead. That was true. And because of his death, Marthe was safe and the children could grow up without the ugly knowledge of their father's disgrace.

Oh, he had made very sure that Marthe wouldn't suffer any consequences. Even Meddling had grudgingly admitted that, with Mercanton out of the way, the property couldn't be touched. The case was finished, closed. The rest didn't matter. Let it go.

Roger halted abruptly and brushed a hand across his eyes. He leaned against a building, afraid he was going to be sick. He was seeing it all again. This morning . . . He had been struggling to lift Mercanton into the car. The Frenchman's head had rolled back limply. One eye had been open, peering fixedly upwards. For one terrible instant, he had seemed to be winking—a sly, comprehending wink. Roger breathed deeply, waiting for the nausea to pass. All that was finished. He mustn't think about it any more. He must never think about it. He must think only of the future.

He walked on, scarcely seeing the ruined port, past the garish cafés, moving automatically along the crowded sidewalks. The future. His orders to report to Paris were in his pocket. He was to leave day after tomorrow. Meddling was obviously anxious to speed him on his way. Paris. And after that, New York? And home? Home was New York. Home was where Carol was waiting for him. Home was where he would finally catch up with all his little trivial dreams of a newspaper job and politics and a peaceful life. But home was La Violette. Home was the farm. He must go out there. That's where he belonged. The vision began to take form in his mind once more. No. He would not remember. He would not. As soon as he talked to Marthe he would be free of it. He had done it for Marthe and the children. He had done it for them. . . .

I I

WHEN Roger arrived at the farm that night, the whole family came pouring into the courtyard at the sound of the motor. The children leaped on his running board and welcomed him enthusiastically. When Marthe saw that he was alone in the car, her expression tightened, but she greeted him with a brave show of gaiety.

"I'm so glad to see you," she said. "I had a feeling you'd get here tonight." Roger climbed out of the car and led them all towards the house. "And my husband?" Marthe asked, trying to make the question sound casual. "Where is he?"

"We must talk together," Roger said briefly. Marthe met his eyes for an instant and the light drained out of her face.

"Of course," she said and sent the children up to their room. She led the way to the living room and closed the door behind them. They were silent for a moment. "You can tell me," Marthe said finally. "I have prepared myself for anything."

"He's . . . he's . . ." Roger couldn't get the word out. There was an obstruction in his throat. And then he knew with an awful clarity that he could no longer face Marthe. He had killed her husband and now he dared come to her as a friend. It was the final betrayal. The house held only horror for him. He must get away quickly. He must get away. There was nothing more for him here. He was filled with a sadness greater than anything he had ever known.

"Dead," she said gently. She walked across the room and sat down, very stiff and upright, her hands folded in her lap, her eyes averted. They sat without speaking for a long time. Marthe broke the silence.

"It's very strange," she said wonderingly. "You cannot prepare yourself for these things. I have been thinking that this might happen since you left, trying to imagine what I would do, telling myself that I must expect it. But when it happens, it's different. I didn't realize it would be like this."

"He was killed instantly," Roger said, determined now to get the thing over with as quickly as possible. "He did a splendid thing. He captured the men we were after by himself. It was later. There was firing. He was hit."

"Poor Jean Louis. He must have been very proud." Her breath caught and she didn't go on.

"Maybe you'd like to be alone for a little while," Roger said miserably.

"No. It's all right. I'm not going to cry. It's not that I'm being brave. I don't feel brave. I shall probably cry later. I shall probably cry a great deal. I just haven't felt it yet. I think it will be hard when I go to bed tonight. You will stay? It will be easier knowing you're in the house."

"I can't. I've been ordered to Paris. I have to say good-by."

"So you're going too. I'm sorry." She smoothed her dress absently. "Life's going to be very different."

"I wish I could stay and help," Roger said. Another lie more or less couldn't make any difference now. He wondered how soon he could decently leave. The thought made him ashamed. She trusted him so completely. But he might as well face it. He had lost Marthe, too. What was there in him that continued to destroy everything he valued most? He said: "I want you to know what wonderful work your husband did before he . . . before this happened."

"That's kind of you. But, you know, you don't have to tell me that. I loved my husband very much. But I knew him very well. I've grown to know him even better these last few months. He had faults. I know that. But he was a good man."

"I wish things had been different." That was true. Oh God, it was true. Tears of regret and pity filled his eyes.

"You've been truly kind. You've made these last months happy, in a curious way. Don't worry. Before you go . . . will you do one more thing for us?"

No. Let me go, he thought. I must go. "Of course, I will," he said.

"The little ones are too young to know anything about this. I'll tell them their father has gone away. But Dominique must know. I'd like you to tell him. And I'd like you to tell him as much as you can of what you've told me. About his father, I mean. I think it would help him in the future if he respects his father. I think it would mean more to him coming from you."

"Yes, of course, if you want me to." What diabolical will was directing them? How far could he go in this evil comedy before his heart would break?

"I'll get him." Marthe left the room and went upstairs. In a few minutes she returned with Dominique, her arm around the boy's shoulders. Roger tried to meet his eye, and quickly looked away.

"Dominique, your mother and I have something serious to tell you," he said with difficulty. He looked at Marthe. She nodded slightly. He went on: "Your father has been killed." The boy sprang from his mother as if he had been struck. Tears filled his eyes and then his face twisted into an expression of wild elation.

"I'm glad he's dead," he cried hysterically. "I'm glad, do you understand. I'm glad he's dead." Roger leaped to his feet and stepped over to the boy. He seized him and shook him hard.

"You must stop that," Roger shouted. "That's wicked. I'm going to tell you something you must never tell anyone." The boy shrank from Roger, terrified. "I'm an American officer. Your father has been working with me. He's done fine, brave work. You must never forget that."

"I don't believe you," the boy whispered, staring at Roger with hypnotized fascination.

"By God, you shall believe me." Roger released Dominique and drew out his papers bearing his photograph and the seal of the United States. "There. You know enough English. Read what that says." The boy started to read, then suddenly burst into racking sobs. He backed away from Roger, the paper held limply in front of him, his body shaking with his bitter distress. Marthe went to him and put her arms around him.

"We must be strong, you and I," she said. "We'll have to take care of the little ones. Go along. We'll talk together later." Dominique went blindly from the room, still crying. Marthe made a helpless little gesture and sat down again.

"I really must go," Roger said forlornly.

"Yes, I suppose you must. I'd like you to stay. I'd like to keep you here so I could pretend for a little while that this thing wasn't true. It's just as well you have to go. I must learn to face it. I think it will take time. No one can help you meet sorrow. They can only help you forget it."

"I'm sorry it's happened this way. I wish there were something I could do." They both rose and walked together to the door. "Just a moment," Roger said, "I have to get my things." He ran upstairs and gathered up his own belongings and Mercanton's radio and transmission data. Marthe was still waiting for him at the door when he came down.

"I never thought this moment would come," Marthe said. "Perhaps we'll meet again some day."

"I hope so," Roger said. He looked at her, longing to reach out and comfort her. He couldn't let it end this way. But what was there to say? Except the truth. The unmentionable, unfamiliar truth. It was too late for that. It had been too late ever since the beginning. She met his look, seeing the torment in his eyes. She leaned forward quickly and kissed him on the cheek.

"Don't worry," she whispered, and pushed him firmly towards the car. He looked back as the car started down the drive. She was still standing there, leaning against the doorframe. He could see only her silhouette and the light as it fell along her side.

III

Out of the reeling torrent of his raw emotions, the vision
began to fill his mind once more—the dead man's face
frozen in an eternal wink. He fought it back desperately,
steadying his thoughts, concentrating on the road opening
out under his headlights. He realized he had been driving
for some time. He couldn't remember what road he had
taken. He peered into the dark for some familiar landmark.
In a moment, he recognized the country and knew he was
on the road to Cannes. His panic faded and he felt a quick
sharp longing. If only Danielle were waiting for him there.
He tried to recreate her image in his mind, but the features
wouldn't quite come clear. It all seemed so long ago. But
he could remember the warm glow of pleasure he used to
feel as she ran towards him and enclosed herself in his arms.
Oh God, if she were only there. The cheerful fire and her
sweet response and . . . forgetfulness. That was it. He
must learn to forget.

If only he could have told Marthe the truth. Surely she
would have understood and her forgiveness would, in a
sense, have freed him. Forgiveness? But he had done it
for her. For her and the family. Why should there be any
need for forgiveness? He stamped viciously on the accel-
erator. Panic began to rise in him again and he tensed himself against it. Oh God, I must not give way. He was
passing through Frejus. He saw the lights of a café and
pulled up abruptly at the curb. He found the bar almost
deserted. At a table to one side, two men sat silently regarding glasses of wine. A Trenet record filled the place
with a senseless gaiety. Roger steadied himself against the

bar and ordered a cognac, his heart pounding. He downed the drink and ordered another. His hand was trembling more than ever as he drained off the second brandy. He took a deep breath. There. He felt better already.

Trenet was singing, "Sir, you've forgotten your horse." Roger smiled grimly to himself. I'm going to forget a hell of a lot more than my horse, my friend. I'm going to forget the whole goddam works. Forget it all. What's the use of trying to make sense of things? There's nothing worth believing in any more.

He leaned heavily against the bar. God, he was tired. His eyes had sunk back into his head, and there were tight lines of fatigue around his generous mouth. He took another deep breath and straightened himself. If only he could leave things alone. Nobody knew what was right any more. Nobody cared. Think of yourself. Play the game for yourself. That way you don't get hurt. But what about your fine ideals? There's no market for ideals these days. Compromise. Compromise. That's what we want. Sure, that's it. Play it for yourself. . . . God, it'd be wonderful if things were different. He felt the terrible excitement stirring in him once more. Careful. Careful.

He lifted his fifth brandy in a mocking toast. His hand was steadier now. Here's to you, kid, he thought to himself. Here's to you and a glorious life in the brave new lousy post-war world. He felt warm inside and his mind was suddenly, mercifully blank. He regarded his empty glass. Wonderful stuff, brandy. He pushed the glass across the counter towards the bartender.

IV

I WAS at home the next day working on some reports, when Roger walked in. I had never seen him looking so badly. His eyes were heavily circled and his voice, when he spoke, was forced and strained.

"I just dropped in to say good-by," he said.

"Good-by? Are you going somewhere?"

"Yes. The good Major Meddling is railroading me out of his territory."

"I'm sorry to hear that. What about your work and the family?"

"I thought you'd want to hear how it ended," he said with an odd sort of defiance. This time, he included all the details. "It doesn't matter any more," he explained. "There're no more secrets now." His recital was filled with an elaborate flippancy. I was struck by a subtle change in his whole manner. There was a harshness, a stridency, about him that I had never seen before. I had the feeling he was holding himself under tight control, as if he might break down if he relaxed for a second. I was horrified as he reached the climax of his account, but I wasn't completely surprised. Actually, it was an almost inevitable consequence of his attitude. He had tried to be friend, apologist, foe, impartial judge, and executioner, all at the same time. The confusion of a whole civilization had stood in his way when he had tried to choose his role. As a result, he had been false to himself and to his victims on all counts. The riddle of Mercanton had grown too big for him, so he had destroyed it. He had swept the wreck of his ethical concepts under the carpet. I wondered how he could speak with so little awareness of what he had done, but I let him finish without an interruption.

"So there you are," he said at the close. He seemed drained by his story. His manner grew vague and rather disconnected. "Fun, isn't it? Thanks for listening to me all these months. We'll probably meet again. After the war, when all the world is reborn. That's the way it's going to be, isn't it?"

"So they say. Look, Roger, are you all right?"

"Of course. Why shouldn't I be all right?" He tried to smile but managed only a hard little parody of a smile. "I'm beginning to learn a thing or two. God knows it's about time. My rebirth begins as of now. You've got my address. Look me up when you get to New York." We shook hands. There was a brief silence in which his eyes avoided mine and then, because I could think of nothing more to say, I let him go.

I never saw Roger Chandler again. For awhile, I heard of him occasionally from mutual friends. He was in Paris, in London, back in New York. The reports always ended the same way. He was drinking heavily. Whatever becomes of him, I would find it impossible to judge him unkindly. There are so many like him, lost in a society which no longer seeks to join ethics to reality, unable to reconcile political attitudes with human responses. I think of him often, and hope that someday he will find a world in which he can believe.

THE END